Fic•tio•nary

By Penny Blue North

Cover art by Sunny North, Logan Schroeder, and Chris Read.

Quantity sales special discounts are available on quantity purchases by corporations, associations, and others. For details, contact the publisher at the address above.

Orders by U.S. trade bookstores and wholesalers. Email info@ BeyondPublishing.net

The Beyond Publishing Speakers Bureau can bring authors to your live event. For more information or to book an event contact the Beyond Publishing Speakers Bureau speak@BeyondPublishing.net

The Author can be reached directly at PennyNorth.com

Manufactured and printed in the United States of America distributed globally by BeyondPublishing.net

BEYOND
PUBLISHING

New York | Los Angeles | London | Sydney

ISBN: 978-1-949873-78-8

For the real Sunny

Fic•tio•nary

1

She was perhaps dreaming, or hearing a conversation, or remembering a book, or maybe a conversation from a dream or a book; on her way somewhere, and she clutched for something. Oh, it was her pink pajamas. And her own bed where she lay. Where had she been just now? Some deathbed scene. It faded so quickly, and now fingers of light reached her and stirred time. She padded out to the kitchen, sleepy and starving, shielding her eyes from the sunlight flooding through the curtainless windows, and thinking eggs. Nothing on earth is as perfect as an egg, with its innocent balance of strength and fragility, primordial shape, the floating glob of hope at its heart, surrounded by the clear and selfless albumen ready to give itself wholly for the potential of the yolk. It can make a cake rise or develop a photograph or become a fully realized living being. Its pure perfection is in its possibilities. Yes, eggs.

On the farm where Chime grew up, eggs had to be purchased from the store in town or from neighboring farmers. Laying hens were expensive and the Smiths couldn't afford the investment. Once a year, in the spring, though, the feed store in Bankston gave away cartons of rooster chicks for free, one hundred chicks per carton. So the Smiths raised and butchered their own roosters, and there was always chicken to eat. During plentiful times, a whole beef or hog sat in the freezer. During lean times, Chime's father would shoot a squirrel or rabbit, or fish for bullheads in the creek. If anyone had a complaint about eating a particular cut of an animal, like the tongue or the heart or the gizzard, it was never voiced, since no alternative existed. Even a sizeable beef roast sometimes failed to fill nine stomachs, and many were the nights Chime watched her brothers pour gravy over slices of bread, plateful after plateful, long after the potatoes and meat had been devoured. It occurred to her, just now, that her siblings, older and bigger than she, had probably endured hunger in a way she had never experienced. The design of a squat cottage on the gravy pitcher, the thick liquid dripping from the spout, and the open bags of bread on the table were suddenly less ordinary. They acquired a new, sadder pallor in her memory. What else might she have overlooked?

A banging on the front door pulled Chime from her reverie. Lily came first, early, and she knew the door was unlocked. Lily liked to make an entrance. She ignored Chime's yelling, "It's open!" and banged some more. When Chime opened the door with "What the hell, Lily? It's not locked," Lily was singing the Cat Stevens song, "This is the peace train! Get your bags together, come bring your good friends too, because it's getting nearer. Soon it will be with you. Come and join the living. It's not so far from you."

"What are you--?" said Chime, but Lily raised a hand. She wasn't finished yet. She pushed past Chime with "And it's getting nearer. Soon it will all be true. This is the peace traayaaain!" She drew out the final note, paused for applause, then shrugged when it didn't come.

"And you're still in your jammies! Let's go!"

"I'm not going anywhere. Haven't had breakfast yet," said Chime, turning back toward the kitchen. Lily followed, still humming. For her, a song was never over until the applause sounded. Lily was almost like the imaginary friend from Chime's toddlerhood, Truly (except Chime had spelled it T-r-y, as she had not yet learned to spell). Chime's parents, who had otherwise regarded her with the cool and sensible detachment of their time, indulged her belief in Truly's existence, saving a place for her in the car, making sure not to sit on her on the couch, and so on, and in such attentions, giving Truly even more substance. They never even questioned that Truly was, in Chime's imagination, a fully functioning, walking, talking, toddler-sized fish, who ate sticks of butter from the kitchen table. If you look up *imaginary friend* in a psychology textbook (which Chime's parents never did, such things being in short supply on the farm), you will find some reference to the developmental needs of an only child, whose chief occupation is often loneliness. But Chime was no lonely only child, she was one of seven children who had to fight for seconds at supper, for a turn in any game, for hand-me-downs, for love, for bedcovers. No, it wasn't textbook imagination. It seemed, at times, that Chime did not understand the difference between make believe and reality, that the boundary wasn't just thin, but had never materialized at all. At its worst, it should have worried her parents, but worry in the Smith household was a threshold reached only by breaking a bone—a major one too, not just a finger or something, or losing a great deal of blood all at once. At its best, it was an unending source of entertainment for Chime's parents, for she lightened their own loneliness. They enjoyed those stimulating panoramic views of Chime's world, where anything was possible.

Lily was like Truly in that the more attention she could extract from the world, the more she herself felt alive. And she could coax attention from the most unlikely and austere sources. Once, dancing through the aisles of the A&P to entertain Chime, she got the pimply stock boy and the day manager to sing the chorus of Junkfood Junkie with her, using a package of Oreos as a shared microphone. She sang the verse with exaggerated drama and pulled the boys in close for the confessional chorus, wherein they all admitted that yes, junk food was what they really loved. It was the first time a pretty girl had actually placed a hand on either one of them, and they would have done anything she asked. Afterward, they had fallen into appreciative laughter, having exposed a bit of personality for a moment without having it stomped on, and thanked her for the corny number. In the Midwest, anything the least bit inane must be corny or cheesy, which you would think would not sit well with Iowa and Wisconsin, but there it is. Corn. Cheese. Food even permeates everyday speech.

"The name is Lily Humor, you guys," she said in parting. "Keep your eyes on me." She meant that they should watch for her name in the lights of a giant stadium marquee or her image in the glossy pages of the popular press someday in the future. The boys made due with the literal meaning as she skipped away with Chime.

Gram came next, also early, slipping through the front door and sinking into a chair with a book. To the extent Lily craved attention, her brother shunned it, preferring the dependable companionship of words snuggled inside a sturdy cover. Complete.

Self-sustaining. And then spilling its abundant riches, as long as you made the effort to crawl inside. Like the legendary food train of Tiding. A boxcar on the Great Pacific and Northern railroad line lost some hinges, and, moments later, its contents, as the train squealed through Chime's home town back in the forties. Sacks of flour exploded and sent a fine powder snowing across the valley. Cans of peas and sliced beets, crates of pickled vegetables, tubs of mushroom soup, and tins of whitefin tuna tumbled from the boxcar for nearly two miles, which was a half mile longer than the whole town. And the fifty or so residents of Tiding ate like city patrons for some time, for the mere cost of picking up the bounty along the tracks. One tiny heartland water stop, in the heartland that fed the nation, was itself, for a change, fed. Included in the spillage were several cases of whiskey, salvaged carefully and immediately, by one Virtus Smith, his brother Eldon, and a couple of euchre buddies, as folks remember it, because they had been nearby in the train station playing pool or cards or some such not-farm-related pastime when the boxcar fell open. With their senses highly tuned to adolescent debauchery of any kind (booze, chaw, skirts, comic books, dice games), they just knew something big was afoot, and went running across the road to the tracks before the first particles of flour had a chance to settle. Virtus, whose nickname was Fat, though he was as thin and long as the railroad tracks (he had been a fat baby with unimaginative siblings), would grow up to be a thin adult and then back to fat again as an old man, recounting this tale to his children, and by then have another nickname. He told Chime that she and her brothers and sisters would never know food in the same way, as a blessing to be sweated and toiled for without end, unless, of course, it fell gloriously one day from the Great Pacific and Northern. The other story, the one Fat didn't like to tell, was about the two years during the Great Depression when his whole family, fourteen in all, ate nothing but bread and sorghum. The cattle too, were starving, and they fell, one by one, to the ground. Fat was too young to process any of it intellectually (this was a decade before the food train), but emotionally, he would always connect hunger with the sight of the only tear he ever saw gather in his father's eye, watching the last of his herd fall, with a final umph as the cow's legs gave out and it collapsed into the dust.

"Ladies, peruse this," Gram said when they noticed he was there. "It was in your yard, Chime, breaking ground with the flowers." He presented a leatherbound volume. "I was going to reshelve it for you, but I can't read the title or author. It verges on the weird, because I saw the title first. That's what stuck out among the green sprouts out there. But when I picked it up, the title was entirely illegible. See?" He held up the book. "It's also heavier than the OED for its size. And note this." He flipped the pages with his thumb and the book spread open like a curtain. Lily grabbed the book from Gram.

"We don't have time for this right now," she said, lifting several other books from the stack on the table, and placing the leather book between them. She ignored how unusually heavy it was. Gram stood and went to retrieve it, but Lily blocked his way.

"Apparently, we have the whole day, Lily," he said.

"Not if we start here, we won't."

"What's the deal?" said Chime.

"She's not stupid," said Gram.

"She has feelings," said Lily.

"I have feelings," said Chime, "and I'm feeling kind of stupid. Let me see the book."

"It's dumb. It's a blank journal somebody dropped in your yard." Lily moved aside for Chime and widened her eyes at Gram as if to say now see what you've done. Chime pulled the book out and looked at the cover.

"Well, it's not mine," she said, turning it over. For a moment she had the dizzying feeling that her feet were not under her, but stretched out in front of her, as if she were floating on her back. She opened the book and the smell of earth rose up from the pages. "It must have been out there a long time. Smells like—" Lily grabbed the book again.

"Shit. Yep, smells like shit. And leather. Either way, cows. Everybody from Iowa knows what cows smell like. Worse than horses, better than hogs. Now, let's get this show on the road." Gram took the book from Lily in a deliberately slow gesture.

"Perhaps we should let Chime decide what to do with the book, since I found it on her property." As he spoke, Lily moved her head left and right in a slowmotion no. "See, it's neither a journal, nor is it blank." He fanned it in front of Chime. It appeared empty at first, but then the words came swimming across the pages, bouncing into one another and never quite materializing until he'd turn another page, and then that page would be another swirling profusion. Had she seen the word *light* or *bright* or was it *bread*? He turned forward, back; it didn't matter. The words grew distinct ahead or behind, as they left her sight, but never on the page where the book was open. And yet the words were unmistakably there, thousands, millions of them. Chime reached for the book, but when the dizziness resumed, she withdrew her hand and moved it up to her head.

"You alright, Chimey?" said Lily. And then, to Gram, "Get that away from her." Gram inhaled to produce his protest and Lily added, softer, "For now."

* * *

I have to interrupt. It really is one of my worst sins. I am out of control and powerless, and I can't help it. It's just the way I am and I suppose you can take that how you will, you can tell me to go blow, to put that in my pipe and smoke it, but I'm here now, so we might as well just make do. See, she shouldn't be afraid of the book, although truth be told she has no business looking through it. Grateful is what she ought to be, grateful she has a roof over her head and food to eat and running water and electricity. There are people in this day and age, you know, who still run to the outhouse when they have to go. Let's not forget about them. Just because they live out in the country, just because they can't get through on the phone because they are out in the country and they don't have all the nice things other people have. Maybe they don't have a dishwasher or a clothes dryer or live on a paved town road, so maybe the dust from the gravel road just settles on everything in the house and they have to dust every single day while the town people live dust free. Clean the dust off the back window of the car so the town kids don't write in it. Clean the shit off their chore boots and the shit off their overalls and the shit from the floorboards of the car, so when they go to town people don't say hey there go those shit-covered farmers in their shitty clothes and their dusty car. Why, they're just as good as anybody else. And they're grateful, grateful, mind you, that they have food to eat and clean clothes to wear to town and one decent pair of shoes and a car that runs. You know there's such a thing as walking to town and not having clothes to wear or there's living off the state, like some people do. I'm not going to say who, but some people don't mind at all if the state buys their food and they live in town and really have no business being there. No business at all.

* * *

Lily said that looking at the words was like looking at the stars, especially that cluster of The Seven Sisters. It was all hazy and nebulous when you looked at it directly, but when you looked away, at other stars, you could make out the Sisters in all their shining glory. Lily had a thing for the stars, hoping to be inducted among them someday, at the end of her long and stellar singing career in this life. The book was no more supernatural to her than her Sisters in the sky, but no less attractive, either. She kept trying to grab it from Gram, and they fought like the siblings they were.

Gram didn't believe in anything he couldn't see, touch, or describe in words, and he spent the next hour inspecting the book and poring over its mysterious pages, while Chime watched and

Lily complained that his curiosity was cutting into their day. He held it up to the light. He subjected it to heat, cold, and steam. He folded down and then tore a corner from the last page just to see if it was regular paper. It was.

Chime thought it was like summoning a ghost. In all the times during daylight when you might wish for a ghost to reveal itself, just to clear up all the nonsense once and for all, you realize when darkness hits that you don't actually want what you wish for. Not really. And you can wish for immortality, but then you can't properly wrap your mind around living forever. No, you don't really want that, either. And if ever she had wished for something surreal and special to happen to her, she now registered a chink of fear that she had pressed too hard in that wish and somehow already invited regret. But the need to know pushed her on toward risk. That smell. When she had held it. Lily had pulled it from her hands before she could say it out loud, but the smell was unmistakable. It smelled like death. And she was too young to be reaching out and touching death. It was time to put on some clothes like a normal person.

2

"No no no. The one thing you can never wear a jean shirt with is jeans." Lily parted the clothes in Chime's closet and went over them with the keen eye and shrewd skill of a Hollywood costume director. Chime stood helpless in her denim shirt and underwear, a little annoyed, since she still hadn't eaten breakfast, and the next sentence bounced out like a spark, and she knew the fire it would start.

"Just throw me something then."

"Just throw you something? Like, just anything? Like a dishtowel or a hamburger bun? Here, why don't you wear this?" Lily, incredulous, pulled a record album from the closet shelf and whipped it at Chime. It was Paul McCartney, Ram, the one where he holds the great curved horns of a Leicester Longwool on the cover. Chime held it up to her chest and said, "I don't know . . . it doesn't cover my midriff," and at that, they both shrieked with laughter.

Seventh grade, junior high. Walking to class among a herd of pre-pubescents, they were stopped in the hall by a stern-faced teacher, who informed Lily that the top she was wearing was not allowed and she should never wear it again. The girls shrank in confusion and shame, Lily having no clue to her offense, and Chime accepting the guilt just for being there. Stern teacher explained,

"At this school, we want the boys to concentrate on their school work, and not on your midriff." The girls said OK and moved on. Out of sight of stern teacher, Lily turned to Chime in covert horror.

"What's a midriff?" Chime didn't know either, and they erupted in junior high giggles, relieved the ordeal was over. Chime's older sisters, Marya and Benthe, or Kitsy, as they called her, were skilled and creative seamstresses. From fabric and thread and what they used to call notions— buttons, zippers, snaps, hooks and eyes, they breathed life and fashion into the practical. Kitsy could design and sew a cute top in one evening to wear to high school the next day. Marya excelled in pleats and smocking. In college, each would study textiles, designing overcoats and upholstery. They would make their own curtains and bedding when they married. No one was more impressed by these talents than Lily, who possessed no sewing talent herself, but loved results of theirs. Now, in Chime's bedroom, Lily fell into her familiar, impassioned speech: "Clothes aren't what you wear, they're who you are." She possessed the remarkable, useless, but harmless ability to remember what she was wearing at any given time of her life, and this only fueled her passion. "Trying on clothes is like trying on different personalities. You try them all and decide which one you're going to be. And the best part is that if you don't like what you've decided to be, you can just change clothes and voila! You're something else." She scraped the hangers along the bar. "Look, you've got enough clothes here to try a lot of looks. Here's dramatic, here's athletic, here's romantic"- she held up something lace, "I'm sure you have ingenue somewhere, here's classic"- a pleated skirt, "and there you are, in your jean shirt, the gamin, right now."

Again, junior high. The home economics fashion category questionnaire. Nothing like sorting and branding twelve-year-old girls for life. Of course, Lily defied categorization with answers spread across the spectrum, but Mrs. Shilling, solid, square, and German (is there a category for that?) labeled her Dramatic nonetheless. Everyone had to fit somewhere, even if they didn't. Chime wanted to be Ingenue, pouty, pink lipped, and petite, in a white flowy dress. "Please please don't let me be Classic," she prayed, shuddering at the thought of smart skirts and sensible shoes, unwittingly foreshadowing the office job she would take one day that would in fact require smart skirts and sensible shoes.

* * *

She is not going to a fashion show, for heaven's sake. Ungrateful that she has anything to wear at all. It is possible not to have something to wear. Some people don't, you know, have clothes to wear or money to spend on clothes. And these teachers damn well know it, in cahoots, that's what they are, over something like clothes. Clothes are for covering your butt, and that's the extent of it. They can all go jump in the lake with this clothing business. What they ought to teach is something proper. What they ought to teach is good Christian manners, that's what. What they ought to do is tell someone when it's picture day and someone comes to school on picture day with a *hole* in her shirt, like she doesn't have any clothes to wear that don't have holes in them, like she's not as good as the rest of them kids who can spend all their money on clothes that don't cover their butts. What on earth would possess them to not say a thing about that? As if I'm supposed to smell that there's a hole in her shirt. Don't they believe in wearing nice clothes for picture day, when those pictures cost fifteen dollars, as if I would buy pictures of a holey shirt, as if I am made of money? Don't they believe in saying so much as boo about it? Don't they believe in picking up the telephone? I'll tell you what I believe in. I believe in God the Almighty, that's what I believe in. And in Jesus Christ, His son, our Lord. You can bet that Jesus didn't care what kind of clothes people wore or whether they had holes anywhere or whether they were patched. You can bet that Jesus cared about more than clothes.

* * *

Chime succumbed to a jean shirt and the pink sailor pants Lily picked out, but not without another clothing story. When she was ten years old, one of Chime's four older brothers got married, just like in a fairy tale. He was so handsome and she was so proud of him, and he married a neighboring farm girl, simple and stunning in her beauty. There was a church wedding in the morning, followed by a dinner for immediate family at Sojourn's, and a reception with a band at the fairgrounds. Chime got a new maxi dress for the wedding, in ivory, with a sweetheart neckline and a pattern of hourglasses and antiqued timepieces and the word *temps* scattered in tiny, subdued print across the floorlength skirt. She felt absolutely grown up. The wedding party and the families were back at the house, resting up for the big dance that night, and Chime had heard excited talk among the ladies about changing into short dresses for the dance. Chime owned exactly one short dress, the pink sailor dress from last Easter, made even shorter by the extent her legs had grown since then, making it unwearable, according to her mother. There were only two fashionable lengths--maxi and mini--and the sailor dress was inching its way up to mini (again, according to her mother, though in reality it hit Chime at about mid-thigh). Virtus, Jr., the groom, angelic in all white, found Chime crying on the stairs because Mother had promptly forbidden her to change into the pink sailor dress, despite Chime's compelling argument that all the ladies were changing and could she please please just this one time dress like everyone else. And, right there on the stairs, her brother had picked her up and performed a miracle. He said seeing as it was his day, it would be alright to proclaim that Chime wear the short dress, and no one, not even Mother, could take back a groom's proclamation on his own wedding day. She had never felt more grateful.

Lily used to dress in nothing but white satin when she was the opening act for Grand Ole' Opry stars when they toured the Midwest. Slick satin pants in a boot cut, and a clingy cowboy shirt with a lace yoke, unbuttoned to daring depths. As if she wasn't already the brightest beacon in the room, she also wore white cowboy boots and an acre-sized white hat that Tex Ridder would have been proud of. When she posed for photographs with the stars, someone had to remove a hat so the people themselves would fit in the frame. She was seventeen. There was that old sot with one aged and forgettable country charts hit who pawed at her . . . but Chime wasn't ready to relive that story, so Lily let it rest.

Now when they walked out to the living room, Gram was still in the chair studying the book. "What do you think, Grammar? Are we fashion forward?" said Lily, indicating Chime's outfit.

"Fashion forward is a misnomer," said Gram, looking up, "Every contemporary trend is a style from the past, recycled for the current generation. So if one wanted to be fashionable today, one would have to be, in effect, fashion backward." He nodded to Chime. "You reach the height of fashion backward, my dear." Chime curtseyed. Gram didn't have any clothing stories, because Gram didn't care about clothes, and he wouldn't remember a story about them anyway, unless it involved the acquisition of some new and exciting word. You might say Gram clothed himself in the more comfortable trappings of language. In junior high, Gram would have seized a dictionary and looked up the word midriff had he not known what it meant, except that he did. Whereas Lily could remember what she was wearing at any given time, Gram could remember every exam question he ever got wrong, way back, all the way back, to before they started giving exams. This skill was a little more useful than Lily's. As to its harmlessness, you can decide. Certainly there are worse unbidden memories to be stored. Question: "Gram, we're so happy that you will be joining us! Will you be coming mornings or afternoons?" Answer (kindergarten registration): "Afternoons, 'cept Thursdays. I spend Thursdays with my dad." Wrong. Question: "How do you spell theater?" Answer (fourth grade): "t-h-e-a-t-r-e." Wrong. This was before Gram had any fight in him, so he let it go as far as the teacher was concerned. It was after that that he learned to use a dictionary. Question: "What is the difference between further and farther?" Answer (eighth grade English): "They mean the same thing. They mean beyond. However, farther is something you can measure, like farther distance, because you can measure distance. Further is the same thing, except it's something you can't measure, like further questions when you don't know how many more questions there will be, or further studying when you can't measure how much studying, or . . ." The answer went on for a full page, only to be marked with finality, in red ink, like blood, "Gram, there is no difference." Wrong? Gram believed, then, and now, that such a judgment could only have been designed to make him feel foolish, because the dictionary concurred with him, and not with Mr. Resch (by now a dictionary was Gram's constant and authoritative companion). Mr. Resch, who sprayed the eighth grade with spit when he said things like, "Are you thitting in the catbird theat?" announced to the class, "Thith ith unprethidented! I have been thown to be mithtaken!" and recommended Gram for the Vocab Club, which Gram refused to join. What troubled Gram more were the answers he got right, which he subsequently decided had been wrong. Question: "Why does Daisy cry when Gatsby tosses his shirts into the air?" Answer (high school Freshman English): "When Gatsby tosses his shirts into the air, Daisy cries out of happiness. Gatsby has finally reached a level of success worthy of her affection and together they revel in it, as they revel in their rekindled love." Same question, college. Answer (in a gathering of writers at Blackie's, down the street from Northwestern University, over cigars and tequila): "Shit, what was wrong with me? She cries out of hopelessness, not happiness. Gatsby's shirts are pastel colored, for Crissake. He spends all this money on real books for his library and colored shirts, when all the old money decorates with fake books and wears white shirts. Gatsby doesn't know any better. Daisy cries because she is never, ever going to be with Jay

Gatsby. He is not of her station, no matter how rich he has become. Everybody knows this. How could I have been so wrong? How could my teacher have allowed me to be so wrong?" Gram, thick with tequila, was nearly in tears. Once again, it all seemed designed to make him appear foolish. Dr. Olsen, who conducted the writer's workshop, put down his cigar and picked up a cigarette. He liked to smoke cigarettes in between puffs of cigar.

"Grammar, my friend. Don't you see that both answers can be right? One answer for each time of your life. You think time is linear, but it's not. Time is circular. We continue to churn out the same stories and learn the same things over and over. There is such beauty in rewriting the answers. It doesn't mean your first draft was wrong." He blew smoke over his shoulder and patted Gram on the back. "I hope this will come back around to you, that you will answer the same question again someday, and we'll see what your answer might be." Well wasn't that the shit.

In Chime's living room, the three were dressed, two with some forethought, and they were fed, mostly. A day outing had been Gram and Lily's idea, a diversion to bring them together, a bonding of sorts, and it had seemed extremely important—vital, in fact—at the planning stage, although Chime couldn't quite remember why. Something about peace. Thus Lily's bursting in with *Peace Train*. Certain conclusions she drew had to be redrawn if she realized the conversation occurred in a dream she had, her dreams being no different than daytime experiences. They came complete with all the smells and textures and vivid color of reality. Time, of course, slipped around in dreams, but then it was pretty slippery during waking hours too. And anyway, the three were already so close that one or both of the siblings attended all the best and worst moments of her life, so it's not like they needed any bonding. They had their knock downs, as friends do. That time when Lily ejected a cassette tape from the car and chucked it at Chime in the driver's seat, because Chime wouldn't sing the harmonies to America's Greatest Hits. There's a tiny scar now where it hit her in the side of the nose. That time when Gram withheld speech for four days after a philosophical argument over a movie. And a dumb movie, it was, too, about time travel. Another scar, invisible, but deeper. Sometimes Chime admitted to herself that she found Gram a little too backward and shy, and Lily a little too loud and scattered. But always, they came together again, closer from the experience. For every bad time, there were a hundred good ones. That time when Lily ate a peach in the car, and this time Lily was driving, and, thinking that Chime's window was open, tossed the slimy pit past Chime's face. They had to pull over because they were laughing so hard, and all either of them had to do from then on was to make the sound of the peach pit hitting the window to launch into it again. When Lily brought out her flute and handed Chime a recorder so they could play a duet, and despite Chime's protests that she didn't know how to play the recorder, showed her what to do and once again created the sweetest musical experience for everyone in the room. When Chime saw that terrifying film in school about lightning that showed how every living thing on Earth reaches up toward the lightning, equally responsible for its own destruction, and she was so upset that Gram had to help her with her oceanic depth calculations for class. Her stories were their stories, at least that's how she was going to tell it. There was no separating the three. She supposed she should end up with one of them someday. Both of them, suggested a folded corner of her mind.

3

The first stop for the day was the public library. That was Gram's idea. Awaken the intellect first, and then there is no turning back. But if you asked the women, they would say they allowed Gram to choose first so that he could feel like he was in charge, and have his needs satisfied so as to stave off any complaints later when their own needs came calling, louder and more pertinacious. Pressed with that argument, Gram would insist that he allowed the women to think they tricked him, so that they could feel like they were in charge, and he would repeat his original thesis: Awaken the intellect first, and then there is no turning back. Each took comfort in the shelter of conceit, which was important, since the imposing architecture of the library unwittingly compared itself to its visitors. Had you been across the street at the Taurus Diner, glancing through the window into the morning sun, you would have seen it in their posture as they mounted the massive stone steps out front – Gram's whole figure lifted, rising to meet the classical columns, Chime's protective rounding of the shoulders, Lily's posturing swagger. You also might have seen what the others hadn't. Close to his thigh, small, but heavy as a cinder block, Gram carried the book from Chime's garden. Gram greeted Gianfranco at the help desk in perfect Italian, and Gianfranco was delighted, motioning widely to the trio that the empty library was theirs.

Gram spoke all the romance languages. It began in elementary school with a two-week introduction. They called them mini courses back then, and Gram's room chose to learn a mini amount about the Spanish language. On the first day, eager, young Gram was challenged with this statement from Miss Appel: "In Spanish, things are masculine or feminine." Miss Appel loved to stretch inchoate sixth-grade minds. She wore dresses and frosted her hair, so she appeared both naturally brunette and naturally blonde. She wore a pin displaying a florid foreign-looking word, which, if studied up close, spelled *Jesus* in the negative space of the letters. She once drew Gram through a series of logical steps linking Zinjanthropus Man to homo sapiens and concluded by asking whether he believed in evolution or God. That was when Jesus and God were allowed to make regular appearances in public schools. And she amused herself with endless plays on her appellation, all puns intentional, apples decorating her desk, apples adorning her sweater. What she should have said was that *words* are masculine or feminine. Saying that things had gender was, to Gram, like laying down a philosophical principal, one with which he would struggle for years, searching for the defining femininity of a house, a dwelling, a chair. Meanwhile, a woman's breast, despite all its feminine common terms, was masculine in the formal. And on what philosophical basis was he to understand *las manos*? By senior year of high school, Gram figured it out, realizing that language is a medium laid down on top of reality. He changed his mind again in college, postulating that language creates reality. And, despite Gram's intellectual investment in seven languages, Chime's pronunciation, backed by little more than a year of lukewarm high school French, put him to shame. She just had a good ear. While Gram was being introduced to Spanish, Lily was learning what made a girl popular. It wasn't studying foreign languages. It was Tim Castle, but she didn't make that connection until later. It was also embellishment just up to the point of lying, but not quite. And she never made that connection. She only knew that whatever she had done that first day of school, she would repeat as best she could every single day for the rest of her life, and the attention would never end. She had worn a blue gingham print dress. Had it been the dress? Or the blue color that matched her eyes? She had Spree left from her lunch, and she had shared them with all the other kids. She must have been a delight. And so she replayed the first day of school in the succeeding days, finding that it didn't matter whether she wore a dress or pants, nor whether she shared candy from her lunch or not. Two small things she omitted in her recollection of the perfect day: First, she told everyone that over the summer, she had gone skinny dipping with a boy. Lily provided no details, as it was, she said, a private matter that was really no one else's business. What actually happened was that she and Gram had been visiting cousins who lived near the river, and they all snuck down to the landing to swim. The girls made Gram go back into the trees while they undressed and got in the water, and they all turned their backs when Gram got in. Wet clothes would have given them away to unsuspecting adults, so they swam naked and reversed the no-look process when they got out. It was nothing but innocent mischief, but Gram was a boy, and they were naked, so saying she had been skinny dipping with a boy was not a lie. If people made up something else in their own minds, well, then that was on them. Second, this proved to be an irresistible tease to Tim Castle, blond, athletic, and early to puberty, which made him simultaneously the best looking, the most popular, and the horniest boy in the class. He turned his attention to Lily on that first day, and for as long as she had it, she was, in the malleable minds of her peers, a delight. During this same time, Chime lived in terror. Tina Carney was going to beat her up. Tina Carney was a fifth grader, but having flunked two years, she was actually older than Chime, and considerably larger. Plus Tina came from the kind of home where violence was part of everyday existence, whereas Chime would hide behind the couch, holding back tears, during the few times her brothers came to blows, Marya or Kitsy shooing the boys out of the house with a broom and telling Mother when she got home. Chime was safe in the school classroom, but there was recess. And the bus. For farm kids, fifteen miles out from school, the one rule most important and best understood was: Don't miss the bus. Ever. Nightmares about missing the bus would follow her for her entire adult life. So far, missing the bus had not been worth the C encyclopedia from Mother's good set, a weaving loom technically Kitsy's, or the Park Place title from the Monopoly game, all taken to school the year before, all for educational purposes (the Monopoly card was in payment of a lost bet to a teacher, and the teacher wouldn't take it), all precious, and all left in a cabinet in the fifth-grade room on the last day of school because Chime hadn't had time to collect them and make it to the bus. But more and more, Chime knew that Tina was going to get her at the bus stop. If Chime timed it right, she could start walking through the barnyard in the mornings when she saw the bus coming down Potter's hill, and be at the bottom of the lane when the bus turned into Tiding. Hurry past three houses, and she could meet the bus in front of the old train station, now the Tiding Tap, without having to wait there with the other kids. Tina wouldn't have time to throw a punch before the dozen or so Tiding kids would be on the bus, in the safety of the bus driver's domain. If she tried anything at recess, a teacher would be on her in seconds. Yes, it was going to be after school, when they all stepped off the bus onto the dirt parking lot in front of the Tiding Tap, where there was no shelter, no adults, and nowhere to hide. "You know, you're getting fat," said Tina one day on the bus. "Yeah," said Chime, afraid to disagree with heavy Tina. "That's what Joe told me." Tina's eyes darted downward. "And flat. Fat and flat. That's what he said." She formed a plan somewhere on the tongue. Chime was stunned more by the glaring obtuseness than the insults themselves. Did she actually think about it after she said it, rather than before? Flat chested? Is that what she meant? And Chime should have seen Joe as the object of dispute, had she given any thought to him. He was just another kid on the bus who disappeared to his class every day when they arrived at school. Nor did she remember the note crumpled on the floor of the bus that had said, "Joe, I like you. I thought you were quite sence the first day I saw you." No, Chime's bus riding habits were unrelated to any of the other Tiding kids, who regularly took seats in the back of the bus, being the first ones on. By the time they got to town, the bus was full, except for a few spaces up front. She had taken to choosing one of those front seats in hope that the red-haired boy at the last stop would someday sit with her. And she also hadn't noticed that Joe and his buddy had taken to sitting two seats behind her. Tina was going to beat her up, all right, but not because Chime liked Joe. Because Joe liked Chime.

"He looked at you!" You can see how easily thirty-something Jayne gets mixed up with fifth-grade Tina. "I think the word you're looking for is 'indiscretions,'" Chime said, holding up Jayne's hate-filled, articulation-empty note. Just what indiscretions are your husband and I guilty of?"

"He looked at you!" Jayne seethed again. Then she stormed out of the copy room and spent the next six months making sure all the other women in the office knew that Chime Smith was a bitch and a husband stealer. Chime can't remember Jayne's husband's name or what he looked like. –and Debbie: "Pateo is so cute, don't you think?" Chime should have said, "Are you kidding? He's gross. I think he has a tooth missing." Because he was, and he had. But she didn't want to hurt Debbie's feelings, if Debbie found him attractive somehow, so she said, "Sure, I guess." They were watching an adult volleyball game at the fitness center, and Chime would not have noticed Pateo at the net if Debbie hadn't pointed him out. But Debbie, like Tina, had formed a plan. Pateo's jealous and often violent Portuguese wife would become enraged at the news, and the news would be the truth. Bullying could always be traced somehow to the opposite sex. Monica rode the bus too, though her path didn't cross heavy Tina's, Monica being younger, and the Carneys moving to Dubuque, where Chime would see Tina pushing a baby stroller down Central Avenue during what should have been Tina's high school years. Monica had three brothers, each of whom, at one point or another, had a terrible crush on

Chime. One even had a couple of dates with her. Since bus rides and 4-H meetings were the only places Monica saw Chime, she had to do most of her bullying behind the scenes, pulling otherwise friendly kids aside to lay out a scenario that starred Chime as the protagonist— mean, conceited, slutty, or unnatural—depending on Monica's particular mood. The saddest casualty was a small farm boy, not five years old, who came to the farm one Saturday with his father to make use of Virtus's tire changer for his tractor. While the men were changing the giant tire on the John Deere A, the little boy looked up at Chime and said, without any introduction, for Chime didn't know him, "Monica hate you?" The boy, on the other hand, obviously had heard of Chime. Monica's reach was wide. Any thought of reciprocating the sentiment through this small medium vanished when Chime looked into his wide, grey eyes. She couldn't do it. "I don't know what she feels," said Chime, and the kid didn't say anything else. As soon as Chime was ready to relive the story, Lily would tell her about the time she, Lily, had to live in her car. This too was man- related, but the coincidence seemed too much. Chime was working in an office highrise in downtown Houston, while Lily was singing at a nightclub on Kuykendahl Road. The pay was excellent, if you divided it by the hours worked, but stretched out over a month, it didn't pay the rent. When she lost her apartment, Lily drove straight to her boyfriend's house in the fancy River Oaks subdivision, where Denton's parents, who had a fleet of Mercedes and a spacious turn-of-the century southern mansion, said that Lily would not be welcome in the house. But they weren't utterly heartless, after all. It would be acceptable for Lily to park her car in their driveway, and sleep there. Lily, who still hadn't learned just what it is that makes a girl popular, did not blame Denton for this arrangement. In fact, she clung to him all the more for backing her in the inevitable arguments that ensued.

"Why do you insist on dating this girl?" They never said Lily's name.

"She's super talented. She's going to be a famous recording artist."

"Why isn't she in music school, then, if that's what she's going to do?"

"Well, she can't read music. It's not something you go to school for."

"It's not something you can make a living at, either, apparently. What does she think she's going to do?"

"She just needs a place to stay. It's temporary. She needs time and backing to get her album out." Though Denton professed only true statements about Lily, statements with which she would have vociferously agreed, she heard them differently:

"I love her. I love her more than anyone in the world. I plan to marry her and support her profession for the rest of my life. This setback is merely temporary, and we will get through it." Lily also thought it was gallant how Denton sometimes let her sneak through the butler's entrance when everyone was gone so she could take a shower. Washing in the sink at the club was painstaking and embarrassing. If only she had heard the conversation this way:

"I know it looks like she's using me, but that's temporary. I'm actually using her. If I can get you to support both of us until her album comes out, I can transition from living off of you to living off of her, and I will never have to be a real man."

* * *

I suppose this is all my fault. As if I was supposed to smell these things. I can't be expected to shelter seven children from school and jobs and town people and unchristian people and heathens. I made them all go to church. But you can't make them listen when they get there. You can't make them be grateful for the roof over their heads. And I worked, by God. Why, I never sat down. Did you ever see me sit down? No. Sometimes you just have to live in the place God puts you. Live in it and do the best you can because you're not made of money and things aren't handed to you. People are going to be jealous, no matter what you have. Tough titty. Maybe people thought you were going to be some kind of scholar or some kind of movie star, maybe you were the prettiest girl in school, and maybe you ended up having to marry a poor Iowa farmer and live out in the country with no running water for ten years and no heat. Maybe that's not what you planned. Maybe you went to Upper Iowa for a semester and had to leave. But you don't cry about it. You go to college in the summer when you're not teaching, and maybe it takes twenty years, but you do it. I know what men want. What men want women for. Men. Well boo. I'm not stupid. And then what am I supposed to do in Tiding, where our neighbors are backwards and criminals who don't go to church and don't care if their houses are clean or what kind of houses they live in. Am I supposed to say I'm better than all of them? Am I supposed to keep my children from playing with their kids? No. I make my kids play with them. I show them how to behave in a Christian way and accept all people. I lead the 4-H club and we take all the girls. I go to Catholic Daughters and the Rosary Society and I teach CCD to them on Saturdays because they don't go to church. That boyfriend certainly didn't go to church. Some heathen family who only cared about money. I wasn't fooled. A girl should know better than to take up with someone like that, from that kind of family. All you can do is live where God puts you. You make do. I turn my will and my life over to the care of God. And that book has no business in the library. It didn't come from there.

* * *

But the book was in the library, with Gram. He directed the women toward popular fiction so he could show it to Gianfranco. "It's an old one, isn't it, Grammar." Gianfranco wielded it like it wasn't heavy at all. "And it's empty."

"Well, not quite," said Gram. He nodded toward the pages, indistinct words rushing into one another. The word *house* flew by and collided with a dozen others. But he could tell by Gianfranco's puzzled expression, that Gianfranco didn't see anything on the pages. "Have you ever seen anything like it?"

"I've seen blank books before. This one's a little worn, but yeah. They look pretty much like this. Not usually this many pages. You need more?"

"No, this one's quite enough. You don't see anything inside the book?"

"Only possibilities, Signor. Potentialities." He smiled and handed the book back to Gram. Gram pretended to accept it casually, without revealing the effort it took him to lift it.

"Grazie, Gianfranco. Sempre tu sei d'aiuto." The women roamed the shelves of the library and Chime found herself among the architecture books. Classical, mid-century, Frank Lloyd Wright, the Bauhaus school. Mies van der Rohe and the most beautiful glass buildings ever constructed. But also yurts, hogans, teepees, wigwams, wetus, wikiups and tupiks. The history of, efficiency specifications for, and how to construct your own. She wondered how many of the indigenous words described simply "the place I call home." Gram could have told her that yurt, in Turkish, means homeland, and is known as a structure made of skins only outside its country of origin. Indeed, shaping of the land itself into a dwelling must have been mankind's first architectural endeavor. She could envision the land speaking to its inhabitants the way it spoke to her when she was a child, and she felt an affinity with those early builders. Maybe the land addressed one in an appropriate voice. To young Chime, a beckoning, playful tone. Pierce these leaves with your fingernail to release the scent, richly green. Watch the whiteness bubble from a milkweed. Sift this Iowa soil through your fingers and imagine it as corn, as oats, as hay. Dig in the slick clay along the creek bank and stand in the rushing water like the cows do on a hot day. She loved that voice and had answered it with ardent imagination. She rode Sandy out to the hay field in the back forty and lay across his bare back, her head resting on the base of his mane, daydreaming, while he grazed on the clover. She built cities in the dirt and peopled them with corncobs. She made tiny velvet explosions by popping button weeds in the palms of her hand. She sucked honey from alfalfa flowers and chewed tang from wild mustard. The land spoke to her in the ancient voice of the Clovis, with arrowheads that curved sharply in her fist, and in the voice of arthropods from five hundred million years earlier, with trilobite fossils that hid in the limestone bluffs. The land was old beyond time, but it knew how to speak to a child. Gram sided up next to Lily so that Chime, several aisles away, couldn't hear.

"It looks like we're the only ones who can see the words in the book," he said. Lily whirled around and whispered a scream when she saw the book.

"God! What are you doing? I told you to keep that away from her!" Gram continued, as if Lily hadn't spoken.

"And it doesn't carry any unusual weight, unless one of us is holding it."

"I don't care. I honestly don't care. It bothers her, and you need to keep it away from her. You're going to ruin this day. This is supposed to be about Chime, not about you and that stupid book."

"Really? It's only about Chime? Then why did I find this book in her yard?"

"Because you love books, genius. That's what you do."

"You're fascinated by this book too. Admit it," said Gram. Lily shook her head. "Like the Pleiades Cluster? Visible only when you don't look directly at it? That's not magic. It's dependent on your eyesight, local atmospheric transparency, and light pollution.

People with exceptional vision actually see more than seven stars. What's your role in this? Are you one of the Sisters? Are you helping Atlas hold up the sky?" Gram paused long enough for Lily's uncertainty to fill the silence. "Yes, I like books, Lily. That's what I do. What do you do?" She steeled herself.

"I make our lives interesting in ways you can't even comprehend." She made a dramatic turn and walked away. This is where they clashed. IQs being the same, which of course they were, Gram had to know everything. Lily found beauty and hope in the space between certainty and death, the space where religion and despair also reside. Chime, several aisles away, heard the whole conversation, straining to catch the content, as people will do when they hear their names whispered. She also knew about Lily's popularity situation and her Houston boyfriend's sleazy plans and Gram's row with language. Listening just now, she realized that each, in a different way, had been trying to protect her. And now she wondered what she had ever done to defend them. She could hold up either as a shield whenever she wanted, but had she ever shielded them? She remembered when she was dating that impressive man who walked like he owned the world. What was his name? Something told her not to remember his name. He was like a dream she hadn't had yet. Anyway, a friend told her—or would tell her, in the dream she hadn't had yet—to be careful, that so much love and admiration could hurt. The friend would warn, "Don't think of him as perfect. Because if you do, at some point you are going to fail him. You're not going to give him the help he needs because it won't occur to you that he needs it." The friend would say it in the dream she hadn't had yet, or she was saying it to herself right now. It was very possibly both. She hadn't eaten breakfast, remember. Chime vowed then and there, midmorning in the public library, or after having a future dream at some depth of her mind that was pretty far down, but not far enough down to remember the name of the beautiful man who walked like he owned the world, that she would no longer view Gram as protected by his grounded intellect and Lily as protected by her poetic beauty. She would not fail them by assuming they didn't need her. She would think of them as equals, kids stepping down from the bus together onto the wide and dusty Tiding Tap parking lot, where there was no shelter. Then she decided that what they all needed, then and now, was to get out.

4

So Chime chose stop number two of this day, just then, or in the pre-planning, she couldn't recollect—a restaurant twenty miles from the public library. People from Iowa, people who are from there and never leave, measure distances in time. It's ironic, because it's one of the few places in America where, because of the lack of traffic on the roads, distance and time are equal, so the time equivalent is redundant. But it's useful in other places, so Chime should have said that the restaurant was an hour away. It makes a big difference to someone who's hungry, and since Chime was hungrier than the others, she would have had the most to gain from the more peculiar, but nonetheless more accurate Midwestern analogy. They hadn't checked out any books at the library. Gram carried only his trusty dictionary, which Chime and Lily knew was not his dictionary at all, but the curious book he had found outside Chime's house. They were in Gram's car, a yellow one, like Chime's very first car. The day her father took her used car shopping, the temperature was twenty degrees below zero, which proved to be the best litmus test of all. Virtus bought the only one on the lot that started, and Chime paid him back $100 a month for sixteen months. She couldn't wait to pull the car into the barnyard and spend the afternoon washing and waxing it, as she had watched her brothers do for so many years. They always opened the doors wide and tuned in WLS from Chicago. It turned out, when summer came, that it had been the thought of washing the car—the independence of having a car—that had drawn her. Spending the day with a hose running from the hydrant at the cow tank wasn't as glamorous as she had imagined. Chime related this story to the twins on the way to the restaurant. Chime was driving, Lily was in the front passenger seat, and Gram sat in the back. While Chime was reminiscing about her beloved Isuzu Gemini, that always started no matter how cold it was, that had a black hard top you could lie on for sunbathing in the spring while the snow still covered the ground, that ran out of transmission oil seemingly at will, Lily and Gram exchanged a subtle, but serious look, as if there was delicate news that needed to be said and they could decide who would deliver it by just meeting eyes. When Chime said, "God, I loved that car," Lily said, "So did I. I had that car too, you know."

"No, I had that car," said Gram. "You just borrowed it at the most inopportune times." Chime laughed in a perfectly normal way, so they continued. "You," Gram reminded Lily, "took out your first loan on some sort of keyboard, as I recall, so Mom and Dad thought you should just share the Gemini with me. A blithely unfair arrangement, if you ask me."

"An inspired arrangement, I'd call it," said Lily. The keyboard was a Rhodes 73 electric piano, which meant it had 73 keys. You could hear one on the Eagles' *I Can't Tell You Why* and Styx's *Babe*. The piano was billed as "portable," but it weighed about a hundred pounds, and the band made Lily carry it by herself, in payment for always blathering on about independent women. There was always a band, and this one didn't like Lily nearly as much as they liked her voice, but all the great rock songs required a lead singer who could hit the notes that bands like Journey and Starship produced. That was Lily. Plus she looked good doing it. But she would have given anything to sing her own original songs, if only she could find an audience who wanted to hear them. Often, when she would bang out a song in the rehearsal basement, the guys would be upstairs taking a smoke break or a pot break and they'd yell down the stairs, "How many times you gonna play that line?" and "Man, that's enough of that shit!" The guys in the band knew expertly how songs should be played, with no idea how songs were written. Songwriting would turn out to be the greatest talent Lily possessed. Paul McCartney said so himself when he appeared in her dreams to help out with a melody or some lyrics. And that put her in league with Gram and Chime. When students were assigned to write a story, and the teacher always read the best ones to the class, two students consistently shone: Grammar Humor and Chime Smith. Lily commanded the same position when it came to poetry. For years, she hid from her peers how easy it was, because her talent seemed odd, not so much a talent as a gift, one she did nothing to earn. In college, it still seemed odd, and she hid from her professors that it was still easy, and, what seemed even odder, that poetry should rhyme. She waited until the last day to turn in her sonnets, because who would have believed she wrote them in fifteen minutes? She wrote sonnets set in stone for a man named David. She composed nearly three thousand songs. Gram wrote beautiful essays, and he hid from his peers that every piece of his fiction was merely a true story dressed in colorful metaphors and passed off as invention. This deception, at constant war with a chronic perfectionism, withheld from him the one career for which he ached. And Chime, well Chime spilled truth into a diary, which had been breached, and she never again wanted to put down in writing anything true. Chime, whose memories, written down, would have been indistinguishable from fiction, even to herself. Chime, with her vast and inimical imagination, didn't have the slightest idea what made people act the way they did, so she couldn't be the sharp observer of human behavior that a writer is supposed to be. Whatever the reason—it was too hard, or it was too easy, or it was too dangerous—writing eluded them all. No one ever actually said, "You should become a writer," to the three, but it was understood. Teachers think it, quietly, and say it to themselves in their heads, as they walk through the classroom: Nurse. Engineer. Farmer. Entertainer. Doctor. Lawyer. Machinist. Writer. Jail. Just like the home ec questionnaire. Everyone must fit in somewhere, even if they don't. And then we rebel against the labels. Isn't a nonconformist the same thing as a conformist, looking at what other people do before they themselves act? Anyway, they had to be something. As they traveled in Gram's yellow car, the book slid back and forth in the trunk. And the words in the book smashed into each other, and began to merge, forming new words. Verb tenses spun. Some of the words become shorter, or dropped suffixes. Some adopted new spellings, and some disappeared altogether. A small, but remarkable number of words took on new definitions. They stopped at a convenience store to stretch and get soft drinks, which they called pop. They sat on top of a picnic table next to the parking lot, feet resting on the place where you're supposed to sit. Impatiens flowers asserted themselves from under the legs of the table and released a delicate fragrance into the air to confront stronger fumes from the gas pumps and the smell of stale beer that coughed out when the automatic doors opened.

"How is the day going so far, Chimey?, said Gram. Chime opened her mouth to answer, but Lily broke in.

"I like what we've done so far. I mean, even if we, I mean one of us, hasn't done what we wanted to yet. One of us or maybe two of us, or maybe all of us."

"I think she's experiencing pronoun problems," said Gram, looking at Chime. "I believe it's a common affliction this time of year."

"What time is it?" said Chime.

"Pronounitis is the Latin name," Gram continued. "Symptoms are a marked increase in pronoun confusion, accompanied by minor possessive and plural mistakes."

"It's still early," said Lily.

"I recommend rest and a sturdy freshman comp course, followed by a fine lunch," said Gram.

"I suppose you could recommend a proper teacher," said Lily. She meant it to be sarcastic, but as soon as she said it her eyes darted to Chime, defensive. Chime noticed, but didn't react. She said, "Gram, what would you be, if you hadn't been a teacher?"

"I don't know," he said, looking away.

"No, really. I want to know. If you hadn't taught sullen teenagers how to write essays and diagnose word sicknesses in your spare time –"

"Lexical disorders."

"I chuckle in your general direction, sir," said Chime. She did chuckle. "What would you have done?"

"All conditions being the same?"

"No," said Chime. "Let's say all conditions being different. If they were all the same, you would be you, just as you are."

"Not necessarily," Lily said. "All conditions could be the same and he could have made different choices and ended up somewhere else."

"I suppose that's true," said Gram, plotting a logical escape route from having to discuss the author he never became. "You can ask if I—if one—would make the same choices, given the chance to relive identical circumstances, which is a moot query indeed, since it's impossible. Or, you can allow for a different, random set of circumstances, again, moot, because it would be speculation, pure fantasy."

"I'd be a time traveler," said Lily. Gram shook his head, outwardly suggesting derision, but inwardly relieved that he'd dodged the question.

"Why?" said Chime.

"Because I could travel back to wherever I thought I'd

missed an opportunity, and just take it. Like, knowing how good my music is now, I would go back and be more confident in the early songs, you know?"

"So you would still be a singer/songwriter then," said Chime.

"Well hell yes!" Gram wanted to interject that Lily hadn't answered the question, then. But if he did, Lily would surely remind him that he hadn't answered it either. So, in his continued effort at deflection, and without regard for any other consequences, he took another tack.

"How about you, Chime? What would you have been?" She looked at her oldest and dearest friends, the one who never became an author, though he could have, and the one who never became famous, though she should have. The one Chime secretly found a little too backward and shy, and the one she secretly found a little too loud and scattered. And, for the first time, she knew how much they had always needed her, how their lives could have been different, had she realized this before and admitted it to herself.

"Kinder," she said.

As they rose to head back to the car, Lily picked one of the fragrant purple flowers that seemed to have taken up residence all around the convenience store, freeing it from the great weight of the picnic table. It pulled all the way out of the ground, including the roots, and she handed it to Chime. "I think we've been kind," she said.

* * *

Well that's a switch. It's about time somebody started thinking about somebody else instead of being so selfish. I was never selfish. Far from it. Why, that piece of pie I forbade them to eat wasn't out of selfishness. It was the last piece of pie. By God, the last piece. I'll be damned if I didn't get the last piece of the pie that I made, that I worked for in the garden, from apples I picked without any help. It could have been the last pie we ever had, for all anyone knew. You never knew when the rain might stop and the garden might turn brown and shrivel up and the government might come in and shoot all the cattle. That's what they did, you know. "Drought Relief Service" they called it. They gave my father ten dollars a head for his starving cattle and then they shot them. I watched from between the slats of the wood shed. The wood shed was empty; there was no wood. The coop had no chickens. And the pasture was dust. And the DRS man had a long rifle and he shot the cattle. They fell on their sides, and I could hear the heavy sound of their slump and the crack of their brittle ribs breaking as I watched. They had to do it because there was no money and no grass to feed the cattle, so the cattle could not do their work of feeding us. Then I felt my own ribs poking through my thin dress and I wondered if the DRS man would pay my father ten dollars for me and shoot me with his long rifle.

Well I didn't mean to talk about that. I was just a foolish little girl. But you never knew when suddenly there would be nothing, when you might have to pick up and leave South Dakota and ride in the back of a truck to Iowa, but you knew come hell or high water that you were going to work. And work, I did. And I had Father over for Sunday dinners and I shared. All that labor on top of teaching all week, and I shared. Is it too much to ask to have dinner on the table at 5:30 and the dishes done and the table wiped off and to sit down for five minutes and have the last piece of pie after everyone else in the house has eaten? Just look at everything I've done. Go ahead, take an inventory. Just look for something to find fault with. I didn't get the luxury of choosing what I wanted to do. Things weren't handed to me. I took a job at eighteen, teaching in a one-room schoolhouse in that railroad stop farm hole. And I had all the grades, first through twelfth. My youngest student was six years old. My oldest student and I were the same age, like twins, one still on the farm driving tractor and one completely on her own. And when I wasn't teaching, I was working for the people who housed me, doing laundry and cleaning and baking and taking care of their kids and such. Nobody bought shampoo for me and soap for me and clothes for me to wear. I had to buy my own. I'm supposed to just give and give and work and work for ungrateful kids who are perfectly capable of working, I guess. They weren't helpless, you know. They were perfectly capable. They could have been like old Dell down at the sawmill. He was never quite right, that one, living in that shack with those animals indoors and the saw going right outside and doing odd jobs just so he can eat. Is that how they wanted to end up? Did they want to be like Mrs. Drukey with her house full of spiders and cat shit and all the kids afraid to walk past her yard and calling her a witch? And she, dead seven days before anyone cared to go down there and just look, just see if she's in there, not a care in the world whether she's alive nor dead. Is that how they wanted to live?

* * *

Anyway, they had to be something, and something for themselves, independent of what their teachers or parents had in mind. Chime always mildly envied people with careers that had names, even the ones that paid miserably or bored her to sleep, because their course was set. The future was scripted and one just followed the script from beginning to end. There must be a fine satisfaction in that, she thought, to be exactly as you are meant to be, to know your place in the world. And she now wondered whether her envy was thinly veiled contempt, and contempt papered over real envy. She had intermittent fantasies about business cards and what they might say on them. "Creative Mind" seemed at once grandiose and inadequate. In the days of her imaginary friend, she announced two career goals to the family at the supper table, and they were not consciously chosen to please her parents, though each could be thought of as the most indulgent compliment to one or the other. Truly sat quietly, licking a stick of butter. "A truck driver, like Daddy!" Chime said with youthful enthusiasm. In addition to farming, Virtus drove his stock truck to the Dyersville Sale Barn every Thursday, picking up livestock from farms along the way, to be sold in the ring at auction. She was impressed at his ability to load feisty cattle at each stop without allowing the others to escape through the endgate, and to maneuver the massive truck backwards and line up with the loading chute at the sale barn on the first try every time. Chime sat in the front of the truck while Virtus went back to unload the cattle. The truck shook as startled livestock jostled to get out. Virtus also worked at the sale barn, in the back, sorting cattle and hogs, and various farm stock and doing whatever important things that needed doing. He deposited Chime in the arc of whitewashed bleachers in the airy, sunlit arena barn. The sale ring sank slightly below the first row of bleachers, topped by a steel rope fence. Inside the ring, opposite the curve of bleachers, and also slightly raised was the auctioneer's balcony, where the auctioneer hugged a shiny oldtime announcer's microphone, trilling his secret number language out to the bidding audience. At intervals, the auctioneer or an assistant would hand yellow tickets to a man in the ring, and he would hand them to a pretty woman in a dress on the other side, who took them below to the office. The pretty woman always smiled and mouthed thank you. And she never seemed to get dirty, though the sides of the ring and the steel ropes were splashed with manure. Animals were ushered into the ring through a gate on one side of the balcony, and out through a gate on the other side with the tap of a whip, and sometimes more, depending on the disposition of the animal. The auction always started with calves, one at a time, and despite how cute the little kevvies were, the repetition bored Chime, so she usually climbed to the top of the bleachers, at the rafters, and took a nap. The interesting part of the sale came later, when there might be a funny old goat that made the audience laugh, or a mean bull that tried to break through the fence. When that happened, a boisterous bull, that is, or—rarely—a wild horse, the whip wielders in the ring would jump high up on the fence or into the auctioneer's box for safety, and the audience would breathe "Oh!" all at once. Chime knew better than to ever place her hands on the ropes, though she saw farmers do it all the time. When she woke from her nap, she would climb down only to the second row, and watch the rest of the sale at a safe distance. When the sale was over, and all the animals had been through the ring and sold, the farmers went home, or paid their bill in the office and got in line with trucks and trailers to load up their purchases. Chime's father would retrieve her from the bleachers and they would go downstairs to the kitchen for lunch. She loved the ladies in the kitchen, because they doted on her and remarked how big she had gotten since last Thursday when she was there. They wore dresses, like the lady in the office who collected the yellow tickets, and triangles of white eyelet on their heads. Lunch was hamburgers with onions, and Virtus would say, "Got any good pies today, Merla?" even though the pie case sat right in front of them on the counter, and Merla always seemed flattered that her opinion on pies was considered. After lunch, the whole process was reversed, and they loaded up any purchased livestock to be delivered to the neighboring farmers. In the truck lot, Virtus would say, "Which truck should we take?" And Chime would point out their own. The gear shift seemed to be the most important part of driving, and Chime liked to anticipate when she would have to move her feet out of the way, because they hung just at the edge of the seat where the knob would hit. The way home was the best part. They stopped at every small town tavern between the sale barn and home, for maple walnut ice cream cones, or a pop, or a chocolate milk. The taverns were all clinking bottles and familiar smells she didn't know held the memories of a thousand beers, and lighted beer signs featuring waterfalls and rapid streams. All the bartenders knew her by name and would ask her if she was bumming with her daddy again. Virtus would say, "I wonder if they have any cones today," and Chine would know they were going to stop for one. After, he would ask for Chime's thoughts on which would be the best way to turn at the T in the road, and when they crossed the rim of the hills and could see the whole valley and their farm atop the hill on the other side, Virtus would say, "Which farm do you like best?" Chime would always pick their own.

"The one on the hill," she would say.

"That looks like a nice one. Should we stay there?"

"Yes, let's stay there forever!" He would pretend to follow travel directions at Chime's whim, and they both would pretend they had never before seen such a splendid piece of land spread magnificently across a hillside, nor a more welcoming homestead. Sometimes he would even sing in his off-key baritone, which Chime heard nowhere else besides the cab of the big blue truck that he commanded. It was as if all things were hers to choose and came into being exactly as she wished. The other occupation she announced was that she would become a nun. While she had close personal experience with truck driving, she could not say the same for the sisterhood. In fact, she didn't even know anyone who was a nun, not yet, anyway. But it seemed like an elegant and useful vocation, and you got to wear a long robe. She thought that the rounded points of her fingernails looked like the stiff headpieces of the nuns' habits, and she liked to pretend that all her fingers were nuns of different sizes and temperaments. The truck driver/nun announcement sent Chime's older siblings into peals of laughter, and even her parents struggled to maintain composure. Only Chime and Truly, innocent of what was so funny, remained earnest. Truly commented to the family that Chime's selections were indeed wise and clever, though only Chime heard her.

Lily played the piano. The piano was at her grandmother's house, where she would spend hours discovering how the keys related to one another, and what it felt like to play with her eyes closed. She composed simple songs, naturally, and as a matter of course, without a thought that everyone else didn't do the same. She was amazed how notes combined, and how, together, they could stir emotions. Certain notes seemed to go together (later she would learn these were called chords). Beyond single notes, certain chords behaved similarly, wanting to follow one another. It would be years before she saw written music, or even knew it existed. If learning to read musical notation is algebraic, then this was pure geometry. She began to see the keyboard, really see it, in contours and shapes, and to anticipate what notes came next in a song by their physical placement in the keys and the pitch she knew they would yield. And she could feel the connections with her hands when she closed her eyes, left hand keeping steady bass notes as right hand frolicked about. She tapped out tunes on the black keys, which she called China songs, unaware she had found the pentatonic scale. Grandma Mary showed her how to play German folk songs, like Du, Du Liegst Mir Im Herzen. Lily would listen intently, eyes focused on the keys, and she could reproduce the songs just as she had been shown. She would never have to be shown the same song twice. If Grandma Mary was impressed by this, she never acknowledged it outwardly. She herself played magically by ear. But Lily would remember later that Grandma Mary's other grandchildren were not allowed to touch the piano. In kindergarten, Mrs. Steineger let her play for the class as often as she liked. She has long since forgotten the little songs, some with words, some without, but she remembers her red and white striped dress that twirled wider than all the others, and the brown dress with the tiny yellow and white flowers. Gram distinctly remembers a number called Jeffry Reed Pee'd, commemorating the day that the circle of students widened around the boy as they realized he had wet himself during story time. Lily doesn't remember, or perhaps has denied remembering, that that song ended her kindergarten showcase. When Lily was eight or nine, a guitar showed up at Chime's house, and Lily was the one who picked it up. She already had a few chords figured out when one of Chime's brothers, Ray, told her she was holding the instrument upside down. Ray was smart and driven, and would have made a good teacher, but he had muscles to build and high school girls to impress. He righted the guitar and placed it in her hands. He showed Lily two easy chords and told her if she could switch back and forth between those chords without looking at the guitar neck, he would teach her more. He never expected her to come back for more, but she did, in just a few days, strumming with ease. Ray didn't have time to spend with little girls and guitars. He was making some dumbbells in the cellar out of a steel pipe and some bleach bottles filled with sand, so he could lift weights and try out for the wrestling team. He gave Lily some songbooks from his room and showed her how to read the guitar chords above the music. During this phase, Lily wrote protest songs on the guitar, songs about stopping the fighting and loving one another, and living like the flowers; not original sentiments, but in imitation of what she heard on the radio: War, what is it good for? I got flowers in the spring, I got you to wear my ring. Sign, sign, everywhere a sign. And there's a rose in the fisted glove and the eagle flies with the dove. Smile on your brother, everybody, get together, try to love one another right now. One tin soldier rides away . . . Lily wove through her activism and romance lyrics the pursuit of the undefined it—wanting it, needing it, loving it. Later, the Humor household purchased a piano, with the intention of sending Lily to lessons. Lily spoiled lesson one by first playing for the teacher her seven-minute rendition of Joplin's The Entertainer. Ecstatic, the teacher placed before Lily a piece of sheet music of another composition requiring similar musical skill. The alien markings danced privately on the page.

"I can't play this," Lily said.

"But you played the Joplin piece so beautifully."

"I can't read music."

"Then how did you learn to play the other song?"

"It's on the radio a lot."

Stunned, but not convinced, the piano teacher turned on the radio. A Billy Joel song was on. "Do you know how to play this song?"

"No," Lily said, "But I could learn." She played a few notes and quickly matched the melody coming from the radio. By the time the song was over, she had added bass notes and full accompaniment. "Your piano is slightly out of tune in the high notes, so it didn't sound exactly the same." Lily couldn't read the expression on the teacher's face, but certainly the excitement had given way to something else. The teacher snapped off the radio and gathered some lesson books. One at a time, she set them in front of Lily, and to each in turn Lily said, "I can't play this" and "This one either" and "Nope." Finally, she set before Lily the beginner book, the one for small children who have never seen a note of music. And still Lily felt no relation between her hands and the notes on the page. But sensing that the teacher thought she was purposely being dim-witted, Lily offered, "If I count the lines and spaces, I can see this note is a C." She had been taught at school that all cows eat grass and good boys do fine always.

"And where is C on the keyboard?" the teacher asked with a tone that said she thought Lily actually was dim-witted. Lily played a C. "Good, if that's all you have," said the teacher with her arms crossed in satisfaction. Lily, who had so much more than that, never went back for lesson two.

5

It had become much hotter, in a pleasant way. Heat rippled off the pavement. The grass was stiff and the flowers in full bloom and the fullness of everything reminded Chime of how urgently hungry she had become. The restaurant was called Cure for Crab, a converted warehouse, full of noise and steam and spontaneity.

"Oh wow," grinned the exuberant hostess when they walked in. "Are you guys triplets?"

"Twins, plus one," said Gram, indicating which two were twins. They were seated at a table shoved between large parties, so the wait staff had to squeeze between them with food and drinks held above their heads. "Terrible name for a restaurant," said Gram, shaking his head and picking up a menu. "Remember when someone wrote 'How's your crabs?' on your locker at school?" He elicited this memory from neither of them in particular.

"Yeah—" said Lily.

"It was my locker," said Chime. "I knew it was meant as something shameful. But I didn't get it because I didn't know what crabs were—those kinds of crabs."

"Do you get it now?" said Lily, smirking.

"Well, yeah."

"How often?" Lily paused for effect, then let out a big laugh, a guffaw. What had been a humiliating stab of memory for Chime suddenly dissolved into humor. Chime laughed and Gram shook his head again. Lily knew herself to entertain the most charming wit, and wanted the appreciation she deserved for the joke. "Come on, Gram. You know that's funny. Admit it." He smiled, still shaking his head. "Well, Chimey and I know that I'm hilarious. You're probably sitting there right now thinking about some word or other I should have used in my delivery."

"Yes, were you, Gram?" said Chime.

* * *

I don't want to talk about it. I've done some things wrong.

* * *

"I was thinking how the graffitore used the singular verb with a plural noun. Now that's shameful." Gram, too, wanted a little credit for wit, and they all shared a smile. They ordered crab—crab cakes and fettucini alfredo with crab and crab soup, and a full-bodied white wine. Chime, despite her aching hunger, could only sip at her soup here and there between stories. Any more made her feel dizzy and prostrate, like when she had held the book that morning. After a few stories, mentioning as much to Gram spurred him to excuse himself and run out to the car to get the book. Perhaps he was fortified by the food and the wine, or perhaps it was something else, but Gram thought the book didn't feel quite as heavy as it had at the library. He passed a pretty redhead on his way back, a woman with frosting colored skin and splashing cool eyes, who could have been an older relative of his first love. When their eyes met briefly, she said, without slowing a step, "You're not eating," then turned her eyes forward. She had her back to him and was gone. He watched her disappear around the corner.

Women with wine in the temporary absence of Gram's insistent maleness: Lily staged her own first kiss in the hallway down by the gym. She wore a pink ribbed sweater with soft puffy sleeves, which were dotted with whimsical holes. Over this, her favorite white painter's bibs. She had said to the boy he absolutely must not kiss her, not there in the hallway where the athletes jogged, and the cheerleaders slouched, knowing full well he would do exactly what she forbade, because she forbade it. And so, to the squeaking of shoes on the gym floor, and the huffing of jogging athletes, while condensation ran down the windows from the heat, the boy kissed her. Kissed her the same way he mouthed his French horn in band. She staged another kiss from a young man who was not hers, stepping out from play rehearsal in medieval garb like an imaginary princess, the better to justify his infidelity. How much more exciting the stolen kiss! Another stage, the one where she opened for a Grand Ole Opry star three times her age, who rubbed up against her and came at her all whiskey and hands and cigarettes.

* * *

I didn't know about it.

* * *

Chime remembered the first kiss—the boy, his eyes, the contours of his mouth, the tingling anticipation, but not the kiss itself. So she substituted the long perfect kiss from the beautiful man who walked like he owned the world, and lingered there luxuriously for a minute. She recalled the other boy's girlfriend sitting in the lunchroom with her hairdo friends, all of them bent close, while the girlfriend read the unfolded card, "For services rendered . . ." Embarrassed giggles that tried to pass for conspiratorial knowledge.

"What could it mean?" she asked from under her eyelashes. Chime, at the next table, knew what it meant. Idiot, she thought. The boy deserved someone who knew what it meant. Lily with musicians and men with accents: A German student on a visa, who played volleyball. A prig from England who was more fun over the phone than in person. Guitar players just like to hear themselves play. You're welcome to come along, but don't expect it to be about you. A guy named Cary, spelled like Cary Grant, with a sweet southern cadence. Every individual thing about him desirable, but the total an addition error. She couldn't bring herself to kiss him. The guitar player in the band who was gross and had a tooth missing and looked at her in a very unprofessional way— not in a million years. His wife wanted to be in the band, but she couldn't sing. The drummer from a famous touring group she met at the record company, when the one she really wanted was the bass player. Dozens of delectable rock stars she avoided, so as not to be *that girl* in Hollywood. Al, the entrepreneur. Al, who made a lot of money, at least by small town Iowa standards, and needed an investment. Lily was singing at the Rose Garden on weekends with the house band, seasoned players with wives and families, settled into a comfortable, predictable supper club gig, shuffling out country standards. Lily sparked in them that old desire for commercial musical success, and they mentored her with vigorous nods on stage and shining eyes. Draw the mic away from you when you sing loud. Pull it into the air with excitement. Pull it down low for heartache. Put your lips right on it, real soft now, when you sing the sexy part. Isn't she great, ladies and gentlemen? If you closed your eyes, Lily, the slight, pretty child became the wise and saddened woman, who knew your imitation love was like paper roses and the minx who begged you to help her make it through the night. She was crazy for loving you and she stood by her man. When you opened them again, she was drinking a pop and heading home with her father because she had science homework. Mentoring turned into managing, and managing meant, "This girl needs to cut an album in Nashville." But without a recording contract, the child with the woman's voice was going to need a sizeable sum of money. Meetings were held, songs were purchased (in this pursuit Lily didn't know that her father invested his savings, and had she known, she would have been both grateful for his faith in her and hurt that he didn't consider her own songs worthy), and decisions were made, while Lily was in math class or U.S. history. The investors went all in—that is, except for Al, who didn't think he could put up the money without hearing this girl sing in person. Messy memories from that night: Al's car had air conditioning. Lily wore yellow pants with pleats and a yellow wrap top with tiny white velvet dots on it and white trim, a hand-me-down from the farm, sewn by Marya or Kitsy, no doubt. But nothing about what they may have talked about on the drive, in either direction. Probably about Lily's nascent career. A spectacular performance, as far as Lily was concerned. The guys in the band gracious to the entrepreneur, who was coming up on thirty, when it should have been the other way around, they being his elders. Al drank something deceptively clear, perhaps gin. Lots of compliments unrelated to her voice. The words "Have sex with me or I won't put up the money" were never uttered. Not like it happened in the movies. Lily had never been on a real date with a boy, but she had been in the passenger seat for some groping attempts at seduction, and she felt him press, and politely backed away. He ignored, pressed harder, she found the handle behind her on the door. Air conditioning blasting like a siren. Messy. Because it was only resolved in the negative. She could say only that she did not have sex with him and he did not come through with the investment.

* * *

God Almighty, I didn't want her to go with that man. I should have stepped in.

* * *

Lily's father beat up the Grand Ole Opry star in the men's bathroom at the armory in Rockford, Illinois.

* * *

I didn't know.

Chime with unreachable men. Turnsouts. Turns out a Lutheran minister. Turns out he's gay. Turns out the Peace Corps is more attractive than you are. Turns out he only wants the women he doesn't have.

"Turns out you married the right one," said Lily.

"I did. I did marry him," said Chime, as if the memory materialized, new, and they poured more wine and clinked glasses. Then Chime was in the hot tub with the beautiful man who walked like he owned the world. He had somehow become younger since they met, and he looked at her as if he alone decided her heart would bounce and her blood would race and her breath would catch, taking subtle but deliberate delight in her whole being's surrender. And Lily was with Grant, who had no musical aspirations, but a precise nose and almost colorless blue eyes, and in bed became master of her body.

"Wear what you want," he would say on the phone. "Got anything see-thru? Because I'm coming over to fuck you. Out of your clothes." Or, "I don't care what's for dinner. I'm coming over for fucking, not food." He was welcome to the jungle and doctor feelgood and there was nothing left to do tonight but go crazy on him.

Another attractive woman met Gram on his way back. This one, dark skinned, and dark eyed beneath cascades of black hair, said, "She doesn't know what to do with you." Gram touched her arm and she stopped, looked into his eyes. He wanted to ask her something, but his words seemed to be lost somewhere in all her shades of dark. She looked at his hand on her arm and he withdrew it immediately. Wanted to say he was sorry for touching her, but words were still unavailable to him.

"If you want me, you have to take all of me, not just the part you're curious about," she said. "Not just sex."

It was just sex, Grant said. He could say it over and over, say it was just chemistry and biology, and somehow that made it even sexier. He left filthy notes for Lily wrapped around chocolates, small household objects that she was to bring to the bedroom after she spent the day anticipating their use, and, once, an audio recording of himself masturbating while the trumpets of Radar Love crescendoed in the background. And then Lily's lyrics flourished. It, defined: Wanting it, needing it, getting it, forgetting it, regretting it, sending it, searching, yearning, burning and churning it, turning it out, over, up, and on, rocking it, rolling it, do-do-doing it, defending and mending it, making, breaking, shaking, and taking it, faking it, trying it, tasting it, chasing it, changing it, buying and believing it, borrowing it, braving it, saving it, singing it, silencing it, waking it, washing it clean, loving and coveting it, feeling and feeling it, laying it on the line, laying it straight, saying it straight, telling it like it is, hurrying and hating it, wasting it, wearing and sharing it, bearing it, pushing it too far, asking it too much, finding it, keeping it, consuming it, hiding it, taking it for granted, holding it ransom, setting it free, existing in its glow, or its shadow, risking it, riding it, running to and from it, circling it, going for it, killing it, leaving it, grieving it, dying and living for it, giving it, giving it up, giving it all, giving it more, and finally forgiving it. Grant whispered I love you when he thought Lily had fallen asleep. The man who walked like he owned the world pulled Chime into a hot dark corner of the city and without a word tore her blouse with his teeth. His kiss was one long continuous search that began at her mouth and pulled from everywhere, reaching inside to draw her from deep within herself. His hands moved beneath her clothes like a virtuoso playing an expertly tuned instrument, while, close by, people passed in the daylight of the street. She climbed and climbed him, gasping into the hollow of his neck. After, they stepped back into the crowd and walked as before, smiling, having never removed their clothes nor spoken. Other times, like the day they met, and stood on the stoop saying goodbye for six hours, it was all talk and no sex. But the effect was the same. With words too they coaxed and teased and pulled from each into the other. He came to her one day with, "I don't think I would like it if you were seeing other men." At such a thought, Chime laughed for all the world. A world that began and ended in the skies of his eyes.

"What should I call you?" he said to Virtus when they met. Chime had created "The Dad Dictionary" to prepare him for the meeting, because you never knew how a businessman from Detroit will communicate with a farmer from Iowa:

Agin prep. Against, as in "the couch is agin the wall."

Boss n. (rhymes with mas). Cow. Must be a German word.

Crick n. Creek.

Hollah n. Hollow or small valley, as in, "There's a storm comin' up the hollah."

Kevvie n. Calf.

Mach schnell n. "Hurry up," in German. Literally, "make haste."

Warsh v. What you do with your hands or the dishes in the sink. n. A geographical feature where water runs off a hill, a slue.

Zink n. Where you warsh your hands or the dishes. I don't know for sure if the German language is again the source for this, but the word would be "sinken" and pronounced "zinken."

Zipper v. To zip. Every kid in the Midwest knows he must zipper his coat before going outside.

To Chime's surprise, her father did not come back with his given name, nor Fat, his family nickname, but with, "I guess Smitty would be alright." And from that time on, he was Smitty.

"Gram found him, remember?" Chime said to Lily in the restaurant, circling her finger around the rim of her wine glass. "He finally met someone smarter than himself and I just had to find out that man's name."

"David," said Lily. "His name is David."

"Yes."

"Love of your life. And Gram's not even here to take credit."

"Yes. What did I do with Gram?"

"He went out to the car to get the book. He's easy to forget while we're here in the spasms of wine and passion." Lily laughed into her wine. "Am I saying too much?"

"No."

"Then who do you suppose is the love of Gram's life?"

"David."

"That's a riot. Really. True, though. I had a crush on a woman once." She looked at Chime to see how this subject would go over.

"Really?" said Chime.

"Yeah. Her name was Kenya. You remember, she used to sing in that band in Chicago." Chime seemed distracted, like she was trying to solve something in her head. "Anyway, she knew I was interested, but she also knew I didn't know the first thing about being a real lesbian. Probably because I'm not. I just wanted to see, you know? She said I could have her, but it would be all of her, the whole package, a relationship. She wasn't going to be my sexual experiment." Chime didn't respond. "And that was the end of that. I said that was the end of that. You listening?"

"Yes. I mean no, I'm sorry. What time is it?"

"Time for Gram to come back so he can pay our bill. And look, here he is." Gram approached as if he had returned to the scene of a wildfire that he had started. And now the fire was threatening to flare up and he would have to figure out how to bring it back under control.

"What have you decided, ladies?" he said, setting the book down on the table, because it looked as though they had taken off and settled something without him.

"We've decided it all comes down to kissing," said Lily. "Isn't that right, Chimey? Kissing? That the most intimate act is definitely kissing."

"Did you drink the whole bottle?" said Gram.

"As a matter of fact, we did," said Lily. "That, and it comes down to kissing."

"It's OK, Gram," said Chime. "I actually feel better now that you're back. I can probably eat something now." Just as Gram had re-entered the restaurant, the bubbly hostess had caught his eye and said, "It's too late to eat now!" She looked like an older version of the hostess who had seated them.

"Don't force yourself, Chime," he said. He had a feeling it really was too late, and he wasn't one to act upon feelings.

"K-i-s-s-i-n-g," Lily spelled. "That's what we were talking about. What do you say, Gram, Grammar, Grammy award?" He sought confirmation in Chime's eyes. Was this the way she wanted the day to be remembered? She didn't mind, her eyes said.

"Mind," said Gram. "The most intimate act is a union of minds. Shared intellect. Sex is but chemistry between people—"

"Tell me about it" —Lily.

"—but intellectual intercourse is far beyond that. To find someone who knows your mind as well as your body. You can't ask for more than that."

"I remember Grant had a smokin hot mind," said Lily.

"It seems like I always ask for more," said Chime. Gram nodded. "Should I stop asking?"

"I know I can't," said Gram.

"Well don't look at me," said Lily. "I'm out of wine. Let's ask for more of that." At the front of the restaurant, Gram handed the book behind him so he could pay the check, and didn't see that it was Chime, not the intended Lily, who took it. Heat passed from the book through her body and up into her head, where it spun and washed into her ears. She heard someone say, "Let her rest," and her body seemed to be in accord with that voice, wanting nothing but for her to close her eyes. She fought the sensation. She could feel a struggle with Gram and Lily, and all their hands were on the book. Were they taking the book from her or forcing her to take it?

"Too much," one of them said. Or it could have been her own voice. The voices splashed around together and she could see the voices across the pages of the book, like dialogue, as if her senses were crossed. A pang of wanting her mother. Then she was outside in the brightness and Gram and Lily were at her sides, holding her. Gram held the book in the arm that was not holding hers.

"Thank you," she said to her friends. "And I said *I* was going to support *you* from now on. What happened?"

"You fainted," said Gram. "Just a little bit." There was one other time when Chime had fainted, a small death in response to the unbearable. She felt if she allowed the memory to surface, she might actually die. So she moved on, grateful for the sun. Sunny. It was sunny.

"Where are we headed next?" she asked, as they deposited her into the back seat.

"I don't know," said Gram, "but I'm driving." They closed the back doors and he and Lily had to cross in front of the car to get to the appropriate seats. Chime watched them through the windshield. Gram said something to Lily about too much and Lily said something about two glasses and he should go something himself and they argued about how much was too much, of wine or something else, about being what you are, and Lily got the last word by asking Gram who he thought he was and who was controlling everything anyway.

"It's Lily's turn to choose a destination," Chime said when they got in the front seats.

"So it is," said Lily. "And we're going to the zoo."

6

At the hottest hour of the day, on the hottest day of the year, in a year that would go on the record as the hottest in some time, Lea gave birth to three perfect golden cubs, weighing three pounds each. Her mate, Leo, took all the credit for this feat, striding back and forth on the wide plain which was their home at the zoo, accepting praise from patrons and congratulating himself on his prowess. Patrons could observe Lea and her offspring on the live birth-cam video playing in the adjacent building called the Lion's Den. This joyous time is when Gram, Lily, and Chime visited the zoo. Lily couldn't see why she must defend her choice of destination, just because the other two had been so blatantly obvious, but if they insisted, it was because she wanted to see the fuzzy new cubs before they opened their eyes and learned to walk, because babies are cute, and because, hell, she felt like it. Just being who she was, she said, to defy Gram. Gram brought the book with him into the zoo, to defy Lily, and felt like a moron doing so, but he wasn't going to back down. What did he think he was going to do with it? Chime had regained her strength and ran arbitration between the siblings, as she had always done. The stories started almost immediately upon arrival. Cats and dogs on the farm: Loyal Pal was some kind of spotted spaniel, who lived to be twenty years old. He followed Virtus's tractor through the fields. Lost his hearing and sight and walked in front of the tractor instead of behind, and was run over with the cultivators. Nawny, a haughty tiger-striped gray, had kittens in a hollow tree. Cindy, orange and fat as a pumpkin, had hers in the abandoned chicken incubator in the barn. Spot, the rat terrier, got in a fight with a badger and had to be shot so he wouldn't suffer. Wobbles, long white fur, and Brownie, a plain brown dog, all colors and smells in Chime's earliest memories. Bandit, with his black mask, and Sloan, because her dad picked him up in Sloan, Iowa, on a trucking trip. A sleepy white puppy curled up by the gas pedal the first time Chime saw him. Vixen, the cat Kitsy said followed her home one day when she got off the school bus. It belonged to the neighbors at the bottom of the hill. But for years, while the neighbors thought it was their cat, the Smiths thought it was their cat, and she split her time between the two dwellings. Chickens: Chickens cannot fly. A couple of Chime's siblings, Kitsy and Daniel, confirmed this by dropping them from the top of the silo when their father was away. But they can be hypnotized easily, if you know how to do it, which Kitsy and Daniel did. Chime was awestruck by their powers. Gram and Lily remembered the farm on butchering day when they were eight years old. Chime's father held each rooster on his knee and placed its head between two nails driven into a stump, and then chopped the head off with one blow of an axe. Witnessing the butchering didn't bother Chime. Chickens were smelly, loud, and dirty. They crowed at all hours. They drew blood pecking each other, and developed a hierarchy of pecking, so that the chicken at the bottom of the order was pecked to death. She was glad to see them go, and thought they were shown more mercy in death than they had shown their own kind in life. Lily, though, screamed when one bloody, headless chicken stood up, ran twenty feet, and fell to a second death. The kids carried the chickens up to the house, leaving a scarlet trail through the barnyard. Lily made up a song playing on the word cut-offs, which was about chickens' heads rather than clothing, and soon the three were singing loudly all the gruesome details. Chime's mother dipped the chickens into boiling water to cauterize the fatal wound and loosen the feathers, and they all plucked feathers until the skins were clean. Chime's mother turned the cleaned chickens above a flame briefly to singe the small hairs. The farmhouse smelled like singed hair and wet feathers for days after. But the baby chicks, now that was a different story, when Chime told it. Rooster chicks came in boxes of one hundred. Peeping fuzz balls snuggled in cardboard that had holes in the top just large enough to poke human fingers through. The chicken house was cleaned and spread with new straw, and Chime's mother hung heat lamps above the straw to keep the chicks warm. Chime liked to lie in the new straw and let the chicks hop all over her. David, in an Evanston bar in January, before he even proposed, watching the second half on television because it was so cold at Ryan Field, all melting blue eyes: "I want you to know something. I would love for you to be the mother of my children." Lily, smoking cigars and falling in love with him too. Virtus bid five dollars on an old sheep at the sale barn to spur the bidding, but because no one else placed a bid, he got stuck with it and brought it home in the stock truck. The sick old sheep had the run of the farm, because it was expected to fall over and die at any minute. Except that it wasn't sick; it was pregnant. David, again: "Let's have one and spoil it." The resulting twin lambs provided hours of entertainment for the Smith children on the farm, and sold at a handsome profit, all because Virtus felt sorry for an old sheep. Immense sows gave birth by the dozens, and if Chime went down to the barn, her father would let her hold one of the pink piglets. They squealed when picked up by the tail, but once held, they would produce small grunts and nuzzle into Chime's arms. The most intelligent animals on the farm, sows nevertheless usually killed a number of their offspring by lying on them. Lily, who never wanted children, suffered a miscarriage at thirty-eight. It wasn't until then that she worried she might never give birth to a child. No one wants to be denied a choice, even when the choice has always been no.

The three friends sat watching the live birth-cam video. The lion cubs nursed while Lea seemed to sleep.

"Are they purring, do you think?" said Chime. Lily sat in silence, her hand resting on the book next to Gram.

"No," said Gram. Cats can either roar or purr, but they can't do both."

"Why not?"

"It has something to do with the hyoid bone, near the larynx. At least that's the accepted theory."

"So you're born either the kind of cat who purrs or the kind of cat who roars."

"Accepted theory."

"Well," said Chime. "I think it's safe to say that Lily is the kind of cat who roars. And I'm the kind of cat who purrs. Which are you, Gram?" He had never considered it. With parents who were one of each, and not knowing which was the genetically dominant, a simple Punnett square wouldn't yield an answer. On the other hand, observation would make the best determination, yet he had so much trouble seeing himself as he was. The lions continued feeding in perfect symbiosis and the crowd watched while he tried to apply some logic to it. He shared little with his mother, besides an IQ. She wasn't the nurturing type. Unbidden feelings crept in and threatened his logic. The night she stayed up with that fish . . . She came to one parent teacher conference. One. She and Miss Irick took credit for what they agreed was his precocious vocabulary. But you never even listen to me, either one of you, his mind shouted, incredulous. How many times he had posted his report card, plastered with A's, on the refrigerator, only finally to sign his mother's name and take it back to school without having been recognized. He could have said something. He never did. And the next semester he would repeat the humiliation. Miss Irick put him in the middle math class. Two doors down Lily and Chime in upper math surely met with numbers wondrous and stimulating, while Gram churned out assembly line multiplication. He could hear the lower math students in the next room reciting the multiplication table aloud, like automatons. This was surely hell. Was it that Lily and his mother did enough of the roaring for everyone? Was it that Lily sucked up all the attention in the room? Or was he alone invisible to his mother? But the night with the goldfish . . .

It was Lily's pet, and Lily knew she had to change the water in his bowl periodically. Nobody told her that the water had to be the same temperature—the water she took him from, the water she held him in while she cleaned the bowl, and the fresh water in the bowl. When the fish fell over on its side and floated to the top, she yelled for Gram. Gram felt the water and said, "Oh no, Lily. This water is warm. I think you've killed him." Lily broke out in tears and ran to their mother. For the rest of the evening, his mother added cool water to the bowl, teaspoonfuls at a time, until it was lowered to an acceptable temperature. At the same time, she repeatedly turned the fish upright with one finger, and told him he was going to live. At bedtime, she was still tipping the fish back up and insisting that he survive, commanding him to try. Gram was stunned when he came downstairs the next morning to find his mother still there, waiting to right the fish, who was now swimming upright on his own for minutes at a time. He never envied anyone more than he envied that fish, and what did the fish do to deserve such encouragement? Try to die? Is that what one had to do? He hadn't thought of the night of the fish in decades. And here he was, watching a new lioness mother nursing her cubs, cubs who didn't do anything to earn life support, beyond simply being born, and indulging his stupid feelings with tears forming in his eyes. He was, most likely, a cat who didn't have the guts to roar, and so he pretended to purr, stifling his roar with facts and metaphors and sound grammar.

"I suppose this is a necessary part of the day," said Gram.

"Yes," said Chime. "And you have to answer the question."

"OK, then. I, I was born a cat who roars, but–" The building suddenly shook with sound. Children screamed and everyone ran outside. Leo was roaring, and the sound enveloped everything and reverberated through the park. It was unbelievably loud, and the people could feel the sound waves in their chests. No matter where you stood, the lion seemed to be right next to you. Any doubts as to why the lion is the king of the jungle were dispelled right then and there, as Leo, not at all agitated, but calm, almost lazy, let loose the sound of his power.

* * *

I would just as soon have God remove these defects. If it was the good Lord's plan that I be born in 1930 when there was no food and the last thing anybody needed was another child, well then that's how it was. Unwanted. That's what I wrote in the family history, unwanted and unloved. There are going to be problems, I can tell you, when a child is unwanted. You have to accept what God gives you, you have to make do, even if you don't know how you're going to find the money to raise them. And when you try to show compassion, when your mother comes home bloody because they pulled all her teeth on the same day, when you try to tell her you're sorry and it's why isn't supper on the table and stop all that racket, well, there are going to be defects.

* * *

Lily's mother liked to trot her out for guests and make her play a complicated piece on the piano, performances which Lily despised. This, because nearly all other times her playing was an annoyance, and a racket, and an excuse not to do chores. It's why Lily performed, later in life, only on her own terms. But here's what inspired the piano purchase: Lily was playing around on the piano at Grandma Mary's while her mother sat quietly, grading papers in the adjoining room. Her mother would never tell her what to do at Grandma's. Grandma's antique floor radio broadcast the farm report in the kitchen while Grandma made soup on the stove. When the farm report ended, an old Petula Clark song came on, and Lily began to play along. Lily didn't know it, but her mother in the next room stopped working and listened. And Lily's mother didn't know it, but in the next room, the kitchen, Grandma Mary stopped making soup and watched her listen. When the song was over, Lily's mother said, "How did you do that, Lily? How did you know how to play that song?"

"I don't know. I just listened to it," said Lily, and turned back to the keyboard. All three in the same moment gained insight, and, during that moment, they all experienced a fleeting joy, which none ever shared with the others, but there it was. For a moment, they recognized and lived in each other. If there was never to be anything else, there was that.

* * *

The truth is, I left Upper Iowa because of a man. I don't want to talk about it. I left and I went to Tiding and lived with friends of my parents, or they could have been some kind of relatives. I got involved. I got pregnant and I got married and the children started coming, one after another. If I didn't say what month we were married, and what month Allen was born, if I said 1949 and 1950,

I could make do. I was pregnant more than not for a decade. I just went in, had the baby, and forgot about it. Seven times. And what happened to that lovely girl who was going to be a movie star or a scholar of some kind? You see, I didn't have anybody to help me. And I had to work. I had to teach because the children kept coming. I never did what I wanted to do, I never did what I could have done.

* * *

Chime gave birth to a daughter, and her world changed forever.

* * *

Sunny is not a Christian name.

* * *

The love she felt for this child overwhelmed her, mind and soul. Love poured from her. She watched every eyelash grow in, and praised every utterance. She held a secret fantasy about running away with the baby and living, just the two of them, in a small apartment, away from the world, and she was amazed by her own fantasy. She didn't tell David, for fear that he would think she was crazy.

"She talked at six months," said Gram.

"She started singing at two months," said Lily. "She stayed up all night singing after we went to that wedding where she fell in love with the band."

"You fell in love with the band," said Gram.

"She had her first dance with her dad at that wedding," said Chime.

"She wore a white dress with lavender trim, the cutest little white shoes, and accessorized with a matching white and lavender blanket," said Lily.

"Her first word was book," said Gram.

In Sunny's face, Chime could see the faces of everyone she cared about. David's bright blue eyes and so many dark lashes they looked like brand new paint brushes. Eyes that showed great focus, but no secrets. Those, the secrets, teased at the corners of her mouth, seconds before some precocious wit floated out. The smart-assery came from both sides of the family. In repose, she was like David's mother. In curiosity, like David's father. In profile, like Marya and Kitsy. She never crawled, but instead scooched across the floor on her bottom. Smitty said it was an ingenious way to get around, without telling the story about how he himself tried to scooch away from home as a baby, wearing through his cloth diaper before he got out of the barnyard.

Sunny's nanny, Chella, spoke only Spanish to Sunny five days a week. In an attempt to impress Dave's parents with Sunny's Spanish speaking abilities, she handed Sunny a box of raisins and said, "Abrelo."

Sunny: "What does that mean, Mommy? Does it mean suitcase? Does it mean pajamas?

Chime: "You know what it means."

Sunny: "Does it mean pudding?

Chime: "OK, that's really funny. But show Grandma and Grandpa what I said."

Sunny: "You have to tell me what it means, first. Hopping bunny?"

This continued for some time, until the time, in fact, when Chime was convinced that Sunny really didn't know what she had said. After Chime gave up and the conversation had moved on to other subjects, Chella handed the box of raisins to Sunny and said, "Abrelo, Mija," at which Sunny, without ceremony, opened the box and began stuffing raisins in her mouth. Chime had been outwitted by a two year old.

Sunny, at six months—"The Act," Chime called it:

Chime: Camptown ladies sing this song . . .

Sunny: Doo dah.

She took to calling Chime's father Grandpa Smitty. And, "Who are those people who came to visit us that one day, that might be related to us?"

"That was your uncle Ray and your grandmother—my mother."

"Oh. I like your mother, Mommy. Do you have any others?"

"Any other what?"

"Any other Mothers."

"No, just the one."

"OK."

Chime felt a need to tell Sunny, explain why she was three years old before her grandmother came to visit. About the time when Sunny was nine months old and they packed her up and drove to Tunica to meet up for dinner, but Chime's mother never showed. Chime called every hour, but there was no answer. Later, after they had eaten, and driven back home to Memphis, Chime finally reached her mother in her hotel room.

"What on earth for? I wasn't in my room," she said to Chime.

"I thought you might want to meet your granddaughter," said Chime.

"We were at the casino," her mother said, as if anyone with half a brain would know that's the only reason people go to Tunica, Mississippi. But Chime couldn't explain. She should have absorbed the profundity of Sunny's simple logic.

At the zoo, Gram panicked when he realized they had left the book behind when they ran out to witness Leo roaring. He quickly scanned his friends' hands for it, and, finding them empty, ran back into the Lion's Den. It wasn't on the bench. He whirled around, scanning the room as Chime and Lily came in looking equally distressed. Time slowed, preparing for imminent doom, like in car crashes and suicides. But later, even only minutes later, the memory of time would be as lightning fast. Why so elusive the moments that our brain documents for us so purposefully and thoroughly in slow motion? Let's give this one words: In the first second, the bottom dropped from Gram's stomach. Along with it fell his composure. As if he had reached the bottom of a flight of stairs, but there was one step more he was unaware of, and, aiming to plant on what should have been solid floor, he passed through instead. His center, whatever held him in one piece, turned liquid. In the second second, he made conscious note of the feeling and that it was a feeling, and that it was wholly unwelcome. He had humored far too many feelings this day, and that placed him both so far inside himself as to be terrifying, and placed him so far outside himself as to resemble Lily and all her feeliness. He was displaced. In the third second, images formed and information scattered without sense. Painful and unjust death, the book, flashing punctuation, the room just then as seen through Chime's eyes, questions answered wrong. *Gracioso*, in Spanish and Portuguese, which wants to mean *gracious*, but in practical use means *funny*. Himself as a thin sheet of ghost. Gram would have been fascinated to know (though loathe to discuss) that in those seconds Lily and Chime experienced similar sensations. Displacement, disorientation, destruction. Of not being.

Lily's information scattered in sounds. Bits of nearby conversations, the electronic B or Bb hum of the video monitor, unholy whispers, turning rubber footsteps, tearing paper, the accusatory rustle of clothing, random sobbing. Chime's mind projected faces behind her eyelids that scowled or grimaced with hideous glee and floated off. And because all of this happened so forcefully and at once, the three reached for each other. Before they could grasp one another (and that too would have occurred simultaneously), Chime pointed away.

"There it is." Across the room, sitting in a stroller, a fat baby sat tearing pages from the book one by one and dropping them to the cement. Their racing to the stroller turned the mother's attention toward the baby, and she frowned and pulled the book from the baby's pudgy hands with, "Oh dear, where'd you get this?"

"That's ours, mine," said Gram, and the mother handed it to him without question.

"Oh, I'm so sorry," she said. "She must have picked it up somewhere and I didn't see."

"It's fine," said Lily.

"Here, let me pick these up," said the mother, gathering the loose pages from the floor. She moved to throw them in the trash, but Chime said she wanted them. Gram tucked them into the back of the book and thanked the young mother.

"Bye bye," they all sang to the baby as they walked away. Then Lily turned to the others and said dryly, "Well, the zoo was weird. Where to now?"

7

It was now to wherever Chime chose, because she was driving again. If this were a dream, it would symbolize that Chime was in control, because she drove the scene, and that Lily was either a crucial element or a facet of the dreamer, because she sat in front, and that Gram was relegated to the less important back seat, or represented some portion of the dreamer's mind repressed, or pushed to the back. We should listen to our dreams, don't you think? They could be God talking to us, or messages from dead relatives. Perhaps the Akashic record, the compendium of all human events and intentions ever to have occurred in the past, present, or future, allows glimpses of itself in the etheric plane. Dreamers perhaps join with their past-life selves for a spiritual confab. Dimensional planes, as explored by physicists, might intersect in dreams, through the medium we call consciousness, which they, the physicists, have yet to define. Or perhaps dreams are nothing more than a nocturnal defragmentation of our computer-like left brain, one to which our right brain can't help but lend color and metaphor. Maybe nothing goes on at all in dreams, but ourselves talking to ourselves.

If it were an argument, which it was, briefly, it would reveal the conflicting needs of three people and their willingness to hold fast to them. Had you heard them, it would have been the sound of three people fighting simultaneously. One for sustenance, one for substance, and one for clarity. Had there been any doors to slam inside the moving car, they would have slammed them. But resulting from the harrowing zoo incident (never addressed directly in the argument), and by the time Chime pulled the car up to St. Cecelia's Cathedral, each was satisfied his own individual needs had been noted for the record.

"Oh God, not a church," said Gram, as they got out.

"How ironic, that you should dis Him while using His name," said Lily, and Gram could hear the capital H's.

"Relax, you two," said Chime. "The church is not the destination. We are going through it to get there."

* * *

I made them all go to church. But you can't make them listen when they get there.

* * *

St. Cecelia's rose in cool, narcissistic arches above the triptych of souls that moved down its center aisle. Incense and wood polish, rivulets of guilt issuing forth from a hollow mountain of authority. It hit them all like that, and the separateness they had established in the car vanished like sins. If the church could have deigned to talk, they might have been able to ask it questions, consider it in a warmer, more human way, but it couldn't. So it loomed silently. Also, they would have held hands in solidarity against its truculence, but each felt as if they would, on some plane, cease to exist if they had. They had felt it at the zoo when they reached for each other. And they were still too young for such fatal feelings, though not as young as they had been that morning.

"I love how much reverb a big church adds to my voice," said Lily, who turned to music whenever something frightened her.

"Do you hear it?" They did. Lily broke into one of the songs she sang at Chime's wedding, and the clear, ringing echo lifted them. This comes closest to how Lily sounded in her dreams. In her dreams, she soared in impossible translucent blue above the rolling green, around statuesque heads of bluff that saluted the river, while her own voice lilted among the hills, echoed from the stone, harmonies true and perfect. She could make herself fly in dreams through the effort of thinking it, but the singing felt effortless, as if she wasn't so much creating the sound, as being the sound. A psychic medium told Lily, after Donnie from the band died, that he wasn't playing music up in heaven, but now existed *as* music.

"I didn't even know that was an option until just now," the medium said. "Your friend just taught me something." People could keep all their hopes about existing as beings of light when they died; Lily was going to become music. Lily's song took Chime back to her wedding day, to the choir of little nieces, their voices like tinkling bells, and the original songs, all Lily's creation. Smitty learned how to use a Camcorder. Still filming when it was time to walk Chime down the aisle, he handed the device to another niece. He filmed the sunset that night and the sunrise the next morning. David wore a different tie than the one originally chosen, but she didn't notice until he whispered, "How do you like my tie?" during the ceremony. "I looked like a waiter in the other one." She had never left the promise of his eyes. David's eyes over dinner at Marché, and all else blurred. David's eyes exuding love when she entered a room. David's eyes penetrating her naked skin. David's Eyes, a song Lily wrote. Another, Occhi del Amore, the Eyes of Love.

Now to Gram Chime said, "Thank you for finding David. Had it been one of us women, I don't know what kind of man I would have married."

"I do," he said, and Chime was right there with his thought.

"Denton," they said at the same time, and both laughed.

"I can forgive her for marrying Denton," Chime said. "She liked the idea of marrying her biggest fan. You can't blame her."

"I don't." Lily kept singing long after the conversation ended. Because she always had to end the song. Eventually, the artist always disappoints her fans.

* * *

I made them all go to church. But you can't make them listen when they get there.

* * *

They turned left at the altar where the statue of St. Cecelia stood her blind watch, and paused at the statue of the Blessed Virgin Mary near the side door. Mary, the mother of Jesus, a poem set down in the middle of religious prose. Gram's mother gave to him basal readers when he was four, that bounced about in the lives of Dick, Jane, and Sally in jejune monosyllables until they threw in Blessed Virgin Mary on page seven. What was that all about?

* * *

Merciful God, please remove all my shortcomings.

* * *

Lily touched the feet of the statue and looked upward. Lily's godmother had been a nun, and all holy likenesses reminded her of Connie, serene and pure. Lily, at a young age, visited her at the convent. The white outfit Lily thought was an elegant fashion choice was Connie's novitiate habit. She was different from the dour old nuns at school. She was like a beautiful young starlet playing a nun in a movie, fresh skinned and vibrant. And pretty. Connie was the only pretty nun Lily had ever seen. Having Connie at her own first holy communion was like having Madonna attend on opening night. Lily wore layers of white taffeta and a long trailing veil, and she clutched a children's bible covered in white vinyl.

* * *

Holy Mary, Mother of God, pray for us sinners, now and at the hour of our death.

* * *

When they exited the church, Lily turned back unnoticed to the Virgin Mary and kissed the crescent moon at her feet. Outside the church, the sun was at its zenith, so that the graveyard in back was bright and shadowless. Rows of headstones sat erect, like students in a classroom. Chime led her friends among the stones until she found the spot she was looking for, a tomb of modest size, yet sealed in a magnificently carved stone and crowned with a lifesized human figure sculpted in pure white marble.

"Who is the sculptor?" said Gram.

"Unknown," said Chime.

"Well, it's magnificent," he said, rounding the tomb. The brightness of the day, the artist's touch, or maybe something else, gave the marble the soft look of skin and the hair a silkenness, as if, upon the slightest zephyr, it might breathe. It seemed to assert itself in the stone, the sculptor merely having revealed it to the light, as Michelangelo is said to have believed.

"Inspiring," said Chime.

"Harmonious," said Lily.

"Eloquent," said Gram. They saw a saint, a song, and a soliloquy. Gram had toured the Galleria dell-Accademia in Florence to feel the exquisite radiance of Michelangelo's David, a radiance that was then sullied with trashy tourists and photo flashes, as if the great artist's work were no more sacred than the world's largest ball of twine, subject to the sloppy documentation of the pedestrian masses. He had overheard a sweatpantsed American woman at Stonehenge claim she "hard thars fawteen people buried raht thar" under one of the Aubrey holes. His view of DaVinci's Mona Lisa at the Louvre had been trammeled by a writhing net of two hundred other curious strangers. Even in the hallowed Sistine Chapel, where talking was not permitted, everybody talked. The only way to be truly alone with a work of art was to read literature. Alone with art, the two—art and its lover—could define one another.

"It's nice to contemplate this piece by ourselves, alone," said Gram. "This was a good idea, Chime."

"Yes," said Lily. "We could be graveyard poets here."

"Daytime graveyard poets," said Chime.

Lily quoted her favorite: "Say what the use, were finer optics given, to inspect a mite, not comprehend the heaven? Or touch, if tremblingly alive all over, to smart and agonize at every pore? Or quick effluvia darting through the brain, die of a rose in aromatic pain? If nature thundered in his opening ears, and stunned him with the music of the spheres." The three were silent for a moment.

"I think I know what it would be like to die from any of the senses," said Gram. This made Chime smile in recognition, and Gram noticed. "What?" he said.

"You just avowed the sensibilities of an artist," said Lily. "Second definition in your dictionary—'peculiar susceptibility to a pleasurable or painful impression.' Or didn't you bring it along?" He hadn't. But he was carrying the one from Chime's garden. He wondered what would happen if he searched its illusive words for *sensibilities*.

"We're all artists," said Chime, with newfound serenity. Sunny at five, painting her own Mona Lisa portrait amidst a busy background landscape, explaining that these were the places and people she, Mona Lisa, lived in, all at the same time.

"Do you mean all three of us? Or, generally, everyone?" said Lily. Because not everyone could hear the vowels, she thought. Not everyone could hear the vowels. Her memory poetic: In the Schloss Mirabell, the Meister of Salzburg called forth from a nineteenth century Bosendorfer pianoforte grandiloquent Mozart for Austrians who knew when to applaud. The Meister of Salzburg was long stemmed in stiff bloom with an unattended dripping nose that distracted no one. Chance, enhancement, like a single drop of dew. She, a weed seeded in corn country, not a masterful rose with a runny nose. Leaves like thistles without the bristles. Soft, content, prolific. Composing pop. Flower, to a child or peeing puppy (neither takes responsibility for a lawn). Exposer of butter lovers. Gifted in ear to word she heard vowel sounds in the Meister's notes that no one else could hear. A was ah. G was ooh. Ear allowed her flair for languages. Sie spricht ohne akzent, except for the foreign dots and stems that whispered conspiratorially from his staff. She might make a song even of this. Already a melody was forming like a cloud, from silence and blue air, bulging, changing, above a valley of lions.

Sunny at seven months, not yet walking, so Chime carried her through the gallery, holding her up to view the great impressionists.

"Bow," she said, which meant flower or pretty, as far as Chime could tell.

"I meant the three of us, but now that you say it, yes, I guess everyone." Chime remembered that the first violinist adored Coco from the stage. That he should have seen her long legs running through the Venitian, not Austrian, rain, yards ahead of everyone else, without knowing their destination. Chime shouting to her, "The concert hall! Adjacent to the Duomo!" and sixteen-year-old Coco shouting, "Stop using math terms!" and all the children laughing at the confusion and running, and not really children anymore. Too much rain in the street and in the canal, and Lily thought she might drown in the boat from the water all around her, and she told the children to make sure that when she died they put some Giusseppe Zanotti heels on her feet, not some awful flats, trying to make it funny for the children, but she was terrified. Earlier, before the rain began, the children had sung *We Belong*, the Pat Benetar song Lily taught them, in full harmony, at the back of the boat, silhouetted against the pink and blue sun. Sunny and Desi leaning on elbows, like Raphael's angels. But this was an autumn memory and Lily could not share it yet. So Chime continued, "We are all authors of our own life, aren't we? And we're not computers that remember every single second and every detail, so we distill experiences and sensations and call those our memories, even if they're not accurate. Just as an artist selects from reality to recreate it."

"No," said Gram. "Life isn't art. It sometimes imitates art, just like it seems like there must be a God, but that's just applying a human need to complete the picture, as it were. The brain fills in where information is incomplete, with myth or belief in sympathetic magic. And I remember quite a bit more than sensations."

"If that's true," said Lily, still feeling the graveyard poets, "If our brains automatically fill in, then doesn't that prove that we are designed exactly as we should be? That we aren't supposed to know, as Pope said so beautifully, the whole of God's plan?"

"No. You're using a tautological argument. You presuppose God when you say we are 'designed' before asking whether God exists."

"I wanted to talk about art," said Chime.

"OK," said Lily. "God is the artist and we are all works of art."

"Again, redundant," said Gram. "God's an artist. We're all artists. If everyone is an artist, then no one is an artist."

"I don't see anything wrong with an infinite regression of creativity," said Lily. "There could be many Gods, back to the beginning of time."

"God didn't create people; people created God," said Gram. He wrote an essay at Northwestern on the crisis of the sacred, wherein he posited that religion and art fill the same human need—the concrete validation of values. The crack in his own argument, he realized later, was that people tended to determine their own values, picking them at random like wildflowers from the immediate landscape, or embracing them as gifts from the previous generation, without an objective analysis of what they should be. And yet they found validation anyway, no matter which values they held. Surely you don't think you're smart enough to know there's no God, Mr. Humor, they would say. And he would say yes I am, and so are you. No matter how right he was, everyone who was wrong would always be justified. He should have said as much out loud, there in the bright graveyard, under the marvelous sculpture, that whether you believe life is bright or dark, you're right, but he didn't. Couldn't. Had he done so, he would have found that Chime and Lily agreed with him.

"Would it be alright to just not know?" said Chime.

And this time, it was not Gram's imagination. He actually felt the book in his hand become lighter in weight when she spoke. He looked at the book and said, "Say that again?"

"I asked if it would be alright to just not know if there's a God, and to admit that nobody knows."

"Not even you," said Lily to Gram. Again, Gram felt the slightest lightening of the book. He fanned the pages before him, not knowing what he expected to find, careful not to let the loose pages fall from the back. As before, words rushed together just before and after whatever page was open, so that he caught only glimpses. The breeze from the riffling pages gave him a rush of lightheadedness and carried an earthy smell. Before he could put a word to the sensation, the book was gone. Lily took it from his hands.

"Hey! Give that back. I was on to something there."

"You looked like you were dizzy," said Lily, holding the book to her chest.

"The book is . . . I don't know, changing. I felt it grow lighter when Chime spoke."

"Now who's invoking sympathetic magic?" said Lily, but the book did feel lighter to her than it had that morning. Lily, too, fanned through the pages, hearing the whisper of W, the words—wanting, waiting, willing—crossing before her like leaves in a stream, and then sinking into the paper.

"I think I'd better hold this for a while," she said.

8

* * *

The List

Our neighbors in Tiding

My students, all of them

Frank and Mary, Virtus's father and mother

Virtus's brothers and sisters

Rita, my best friend

Joanne, my sister, and her children

My dearest brother Rick, and his family

Mother and Father

Allen

Virtus, Jr.

Marya

Ray

Benthe

Daniel

Chime

Virtus

Myself

* * *

Afternoon clouds tumbled in and the day grew cooler. They left St. Cecelia, a hollow polyresin statue made in a factory in New Mexico, presiding over the silent church, and the human marble figure breathed into life by an unknown artist, presiding over the church's equally silent former parishioners. They stood on the steps of St. Cecelia's Cathedral discussing possibilities. You would think that among the three friends, someone would have made a plan for the next destination, but none had, at least not that memory supplied. Then Gram, chiding himself for not having thought of it that morning, decided that they should weigh the book. Without an initial measurement, the control on the experiment would be specious, but at least they would have a definitive number for comparison going forward. They needed only to travel to the nearest grocery store with a produce department, where they could find scales. Lily agreed, as long as the grocery store also had a liquor department and she would be the one to handle the book. Chime said she would be happy if the store had a restroom. They found a HyVee just down the street, across from another church and next to a bar, and Lily said, "Geez, Iowa," because in Iowa, it is said that there's a church and a bar on every corner of every town. Smitty liked to go to the meetings in the basement of the Doghouse Saloon (at the corner of University and Ashton Road, across from St. Thomas Aquinas). Tuesdays were AA meetings, and Thursdays were Gambler's Anonymous meetings. He said the alcoholics liked to gamble and the reformed gamblers liked to drink, so a guy could get the best of both worlds if he went Tuesdays and Thursdays. Smitty also liked to play poker in the back room of the Union Cigar Store, where the card game was once held up by two armed men. The robbers made the card players remove their pants, thereby collecting their wallets, weapons, and a few extra minutes of getaway time while the bare-legged men weighed their nudity against giving chase. Taken in the contents of Smitty's pants was a small wrinkled note that said "Daddy, Love Forever, Your Little Girl, Chimey" from fifteen years earlier. After that, Smitty carried his gun in his boot. Chime at Neiman Marcus, offering credit cards for payment: "I also carry a 'Greatest-mommy-in-the-world' card, if that will get me anything." Gram's exchanges with Hy-Vee checkers when he moved back to Iowa:

Checker: Do you have a HyVee fuelsaver card at all?

Gram: Not even a little bit.

Checker: Were these avocadoes?

Gram: As far as I know, they've always been avocadoes.

Checker: Did you want paper or plastic?

Gram: No, I didn't.

Checker: Could you give me a good phone number?

Gram: Yes. 555-5555 is easy to remember. How about 867-5309? Both are good.

They took the book to the produce department and Lily placed it on the scale. The needle spun around and landed almost back where it had been. According to the scale, the book weighed less than four ounces, which was the mark just to the right of zero. The three held each other's eyes for a moment in silent witness, and then Lily took back the book, holding it to her chest. Chime said she was going to find the bathroom and Lily said she and Gram would be in the liquor aisle. When Chime was gone, Gram grabbed a five-pound bag of potatoes and handed it to Lily.

"Which is heavier?" he said. Lily's limbs looked like a pair of balancing scales, as she moved the specimens up and down for comparison.

"They feel about the same," she said.

"That's what I would have guessed," said Gram.

"I also would have guessed that it weighed at least six pounds this morning." He replaced the potatoes and guided Lily by the arm, resisting the dizziness that seemed to pass from the book and through Lily to his brain. "And I'll tell you something else." They walked toward the sign that read "Spirits." "It's starting to affect me the way it affects her. I can feel it right now, just touching your arm."

"What did you expect?"

"I don't know. I thought today was all about her. But I know that this morning I was logical and reasonable, and in control. And now . . . now I feel like I'm losing myself." Lily didn't want to admit a brush with the same sensation. She shrugged his hand away. They turned down the liquor aisle. "Don't you find it odd that none of us can remember where we were supposed to go next? On a day that we planned months ago?"

"I thought we planned it yesterday."

"Really? Tell me, then. Where were you yesterday?"

"With the two of you, at the cathedral," said Lily. Gram's face turned ashen.

"Look, Lily," he said. "If anything strange were to happen to us, to me, if I had some kind of accident—God!—or if one of us were to just, I don't know, disappear, please remember that I said this. I love you." Lily's eyes widened. "I love you and I love Chime and I don't think I would be anything without the two of you," and he didn't know if he had used the right pronoun. "The two of them." Images of David and Sunny shot through both of them.

"I'll remember," said Lily, and she was moved and frightened by his words, but also by the feeling of the book in her hand. It had grown lighter as he spoke, as if he had pulled the words from the book itself and by releasing them into the air, lightened its load.

Chime, in the days of her imaginary friend, to her parents: "When I get big, and you get little, then things are going to be different."

Truly, licking butter from her fins: "Wise and clever choices, indeed."

A petite blonde entered the aisle to study the rum selection. For a second, Lily and Gram thought they recognized her as a high school friend. She must have felt their gaze, because she turned to meet it with a bottle in her hand.

"I highly recommend the Rumchata, if you're trying to decide," she said.

"Oh, we weren't—" Gram started.

"Yes, we were," said Lily. "He'll take two." The woman handed Gram her bottle and another from the shelf and flashed a brilliant smile.

"Pardon me, but is your name Jolie?" said Gram.

"Um, no . . ." she said, though she seemed uncertain. "What time is it?" The twins looked at each other.

"There's been some disagreement on that," said Lily. "We're not sure."

"Oh. I left my phone somewhere so I don't know either," she said, looking around, as if for her phone. Jolie's dad answering the door with "Smitty! How the hell are ya! Sonofabitch you're a tall one! How's your ol' man? I saw him up at Breitbach's. Playin' the euchre tournament. Man, it was hotter than a two-bit whore in there and there's Smitty at the first table, givin' 'em a piss poundin.' Does that sonofabitch ever lose?"

"Whatcha got there?" she asked, eyeing the book in Lily's arms. Lily handed her the book, and she took it like it weighed nothing at all.

"Oh, a journal! I love these things! I think I filled a hundred of them when I was a teenager. You know, lots of superlatives and angst, adolescent stuff."

"Why don't you keep this one," Lily suggested. Gram opened his mouth to protest, but nothing came out. "We're getting tired of carrying it around." Carrying Jolie around on the playground at school. She weighed only eighty pounds, so it was easy to make her fly.

"Let's play Helen Keller again. You be Helen and I'll be the Miracle Worker."

"Oh no, I couldn't. This is yours." She handed the book back to Lily, and suddenly she was in a hurry. "You know what? I'm early. I mean, I'm late. For a party. It's at Derby Grange, out on the archery range. You should come. See you there?" Possibly-Jolie ran off empty handed, shouting, "Just keep following the road north!"

As soon as the woman was out of sight, Chime appeared. "Watch this," Gram whispered to Lily. "Chime, guess who we just saw."

"I don't know, a sailor?" Chime pointed her eyes to Gram's bottles of rum.

"A sailor's daughter," said Lily. "Jolie."

Chime wheeled around in search of traces, a scent or sight. "What's she doing here? Did you tell her I was here? Why did she leave?" She left when she got married. Moved to Wyoming and then Kentucky. Since it was during the same years as the ill-fated Denton marriage, opportunities to see Jolie were rare. And whenever a husband pits his wife against her family and friends, because he's "the only one who really cares about you," as was the case for both, the wives should run for the hills. Instead, they dragged themselves away slowly and painfully. The day Sunny was born, Chime turned to David and said, "We're going to have to move," because she couldn't visualize raising a child anywhere south of Chicago. They say that everyone comes back, eventually, to Iowa. It could be the beauty of the rolling hills and sharp bluffs, the grandeur of the Mississippi River, the clean air, the smell of fresh-cut clover and hay. Where the only thing that might cause a traffic jam is a slow-moving tractor. Where no one has ever seen a celebrity, and doesn't care to. Something, the air, the soil, the sense, gets into you and never goes away. She had wanted Sunny's newborn feet to first touch Iowa soil, so Kitsy sent some dirt in a small jar.

"You don't know?" said Gram.

"How would I know?" said Chime. "I was in the bathroom!"

"It was someone who looked like Jolie, anyway" said Lily.

"Well was it Jolie or not?" said Chime, and they realized Chime was as bewildered as they.

"Let's get out of here," said Gram. "We need some fresh air." Lily said she really really needed that rum about now, and that she would pay for it and meet them outside. She set the book down on the grocery shelf and Gram handed her the bottles. She picked up the book and made sure Gram had seen, and when he and Chime turned away she returned it to the shelf.

"Goodbye, strange book," she said, and headed for checkout. Outside in the parking lot, Chime leaned against the car and Gram faced her, as he tried to account for the strange happenings of the day. Or whatever amount of time had passed. A breeze cooled the air, shuddered the tree above them, and carried the scent of clover, of hay. From a distance, it looked like Chime could have been crying. Sunny, fourth grade, on a crying jag. She couldn't stop. She cried through breakfast and dressing, through packing her backpack and getting in the car. Chime held her close in the car, parked near the side door of the school, and sang softly into her hair. It had to be hormones, she thought, harbingers of great physical change to follow. And it was all she could do to keep from crying herself. Give it to me, give all the sadness to me, she pleaded with the universe. Chime with tears running down her face as she watched David's car down the driveway. He left that day, as he had for some time, without a kiss, without a word. The day after Sunny's sixteenth birthday, he came home in the middle of the day. To talk. Things couldn't go on as they were, he said. They had to get better, or he had to leave, but either way they had to change. And Chime said this can't be real.

"I think she had so much potential, she wanted to do so many great things, but she found herself married, raising children instead, and I think she blamed it on her husband," said Aunt Joanne. Chime, Marya, and Kitsy sat in Joanne's bright kitchen, surrounded by cousins they hadn't seen since childhood, and began to see their mother through her sister's eyes. She, their mother, had been at the gravesite, looking small in a black coat, and disappearing without acknowledging anyone, even her daughters. Joanne produced old photographs taken on a summer visit to the farm. There were all the Smith children, Allen and Virtus, Jr. in open plaid shirts with the sleeves cut off, showing off new teenage muscles, and Ray in imitation of the older boys. Daniel taller than Kitsy, though she was older, and their arms around each other, looking happy and playworn. Everyone tan from making hay (except for Virtus's forehead, as all farmers, kept perennially white by his hat). They were gathered around their smiling parents, with five-year-old Chime at her mother's feet and Marya, also a teenager, resting a maternal hand on Chime's shoulder. Chime had no memory of Joanne ever visiting, nor of the sisters ever speaking. But they must have been close at some point.

* * *

She said she was going to be a singer, she didn't need to go to college.

* * *

Sunny, at Chime's feet with her sophomore English textbook, and Chime holding onto the present moment like fragile glass.

"Why so much focus on the crumbling state of the stones, do you think?" said Chime, keeping her voice steady, for Sunny. David said they looked so close like that.

"Poe uses the stones as a symbol for the crumbling House of Usher." He could leave knowing Chime would always be a good mother.

"Good. But you need to go deeper." For Sunny. For Sunny. Pretend the world isn't ending.

"But that's the answer the teacher is looking for, Mom." He said he loved Chime, but not this.

"Are you learning just enough to please the teacher?" Because he loves me, but not this. What is this?

"It's enough."

"It's not enough."

It's not enough. Gram took Chime's hand and tried to live the memory with her, but it didn't seem he was much help. Chime thought for a while that the man who walked like he owned the world, the man with the eyes of love, was someone she made up. And when he ceased to conform to her definition, when he became a real, separate man, she didn't recognize him. The world spun. Don't think of him as perfect. Because if you do, at some point you are going to fail him. You're not going to give him the help he needs because it won't occur to you that he needs it. A friend had said it in a dream once, or she was saying it to herself right now. It was very possibly both. She walked through the house while Sunny was at school and touched the furniture, the curtains, the photographs, making sure everything was solid. There was a book where they would write to each other every year on their wedding anniversary. It seemed to be missing. When had they stopped writing, and stopped looking for each other's messages? The book was gone, and with it, years. Suddenly, finding that book became crucial, as if its existence proved reality. Frantic, she tore up the living room. She looked under beds and on bookshelves. She wrung her brain for a memory of anything they had written, but only two small drops fell into her consciousness. He had written "I miss you" the year after Sunny was born. And she had written "The shining thing called me gets smaller" . . . when? And, because the two lines were all she could remember, they took on new meaning next to each other. They made her think that it was herself who was made up and ill-defined. Someone she had wanted to be, who materialized initially, and had been shrinking ever since, until David couldn't see her anymore. Lily's immediate ache was for the songs. The life would be ripped from them if he left, leaving hollow shells, ghosts in pretty clothes. She didn't think she could ever sing them again. Gram had nothing to say on the subject, and so he stood by helplessly. But now, in the HyVee parking lot, with Chime's story, Gram had changed. As much as his own emotions had always frightened him, today they had announced themselves and their plans to hang around. And though they tore away at his identity, they also gave him new understanding of his sister and his friend. Of course. He didn't know why he hadn't realized it before. If Lily had looked objectively, rather than artistically, at her own lyrics, she would have seen a chronicle of her life. It was all written down, plain and logical as an essay. The artist and the art lover hold eternity in a single moment. Individual moments cease to exist for them. So the songs were never single moments or the mere capture of an emotion, as he had been taught, but a small space holding all of time. Meaningless, if time were removed. As for Chime, her blinding sorrow at the thought of Dave leaving had made Gram invisible, but Gram could have helped. She too held all of time in a single moment, and he could have, should have, found Chime's counterpart to Lily's lyrics. Gram would have made the connection between "I miss you" and "The shining thing called me gets smaller" no matter how many words came between. In that he was an expert.

Now he laced his fingers with hers and said, "Worst day of our life, certainly. Had I helped you, it might not have been necessary."

"I wouldn't have listened to you," said Chime.

"What? But I know practically everything!" Gram exaggerated pretend injury, which made Chime smile.

"But you're kind of an ass," she said, and they both laughed.

According to Sunny, two years old, interviewed by Chime:

How old is Daddy?

Two.

How old is Mommy?

Two.

How old is Grandma?

Two.

How old is Grandpa?

Two.

How old is Chella?

Three.

What is Daddy's job?

Golf.

What is Daddy's favorite thing?

A present with a bow.

Whom does Daddy love?

You, mommy. And me. And my new train.

Where does Santa Clause live?

In a book.

Where do your ideas come from?

I eat. Then I do a project.

What are you going to be when you grow up?

I'm not growing up.

If you could give Daddy anything in the whole world, what would it be?

His birthday hat.

What is the most important thing in life?

My bottle with the milk in it.

What is Mommy's job? Be happy all the time, never get tired, and push me on my swing.

Lily brought two bottles of Rumchata and plastic cups in a paper grocery bag to the car, and suggested they start drinking immediately. Chime, visiting Smitty at his log cabin after the divorce: "Got anything to drink? I've just been to Mother's." He was making homemade wine in the basement, and poured some fuel-smelling liquid into a water glass. Made from melons and tomatoes from his garden. And he was leaving surplus from his harvest on the porch every morning for an orphaned baby fox. Because he was always going to be some kind of farmer, no matter how old, growing something, feeding something, turning what nature offered into something more. Chime, at lunch before Sunny's piano recital, sending a group text.

"It's 11:30 and I'm with my mother at lunch. Too early to drink?" She had helped Sunny with her hair bow earlier, turning her around from the mirror to look into her eyes.

"You should know that Grandma Smith has always been a very negative person."

"OK."

"She might find something wrong with your dress, or your performance, but it won't be true. It will just be some of the bad feelings she carries around, OK?"

"OK."

"Her new husband's name is Charles."

"OK." And then Sunny entered the kitchen to find her grandmother reading the homework notebook she had left open on the counter. Sunny had not seen her in five years, since that first time in Memphis.

"How do you spell conscientious?" she said by way of greeting.

"Excuse me?" said Sunny.

"It's spelled wrong here," she said, pointing disapprovingly to the notebook. And then Dave became aware of something that needed fixing in the house, so he said to go on to lunch without him and that he would be at the recital. The text answers came in with rapidity. From Jolie, "My mom is coming on Sunday and I started drinking Thursday!" From Karen, "Anytime is bloody mary time!" What the hell, she ordered a bloody mary while her mother told Charles what he wanted to eat.

The wind lifted leaves from the trees and they floated randomly until the ground settled them. Gram was thinking how pages and leaves referred to the same thing, how leaves could be the obvious lateral outgrowths people expected, the way they were always depicted, or they could be something else, the scientific designations escaping him, something else entirely. What the something else was called didn't seem to matter like it would have that morning. He gave himself fully to the leaves. He was a leaf. Wanted a leaf. He reached for some in the maple tree's hesitant yellow-gold shower, and they changed directions for no reason, eluding him. He reached for more, and caught a few pointed edges briefly before they slipped through his fingers. Then he followed just one leaf, trailing it with his eyes wherever it led, keeping his hands open, until finally, it landed gently in his palm, as if that were its destination all along. Lily and Chime watched with the wonder of children. Leaves. Harbingers of great physical changes to come. They moved into the car and the women drank Rumchata in the back seat, which reminded them of Grandma's homemade rice pudding, and so it warmed them in two ways.

When he thought the time was right, Gram said, "I think we should talk about Willa, all three of us."

9

"I don't think I bought enough booze," said Lily. "You know, there's a party at Derby Grange . . ."

"Chime, we need to do this. Agreed?"

"What time is it?" said Chime.

"It's starting to get late," said Gram. "Look at the leaves."

"Alright," she said, though she felt like she had forgotten to do something.

"Lily?" Lily peered into her drink and summoned a song from its deceptive sweetness. Is this the real life? Is this just fantasy? Caught in a landslide, no escape from reality. Open your eyes, look up to the skies and see. I'm just a poor boy, I need no sympathy, because I'm easy come, easy go, little high, little low. Any way the wind blows doesn't really matter to me. Except it did matter to her, and she could feel herself disappearing, like Gram did before the leaves started falling.

"It has to be done together," said Gram.

"Everyone jump upon the peace train . . . Well I'm not ready. I said there's a party at Derby Grange and we were invited and we should go."

For heaven's sake, I'm dead. Dried up and blown away. Don't you think I want a little peace as well? I'm floored. I'm worded to death. I've said everything I want to say. I put myself in God's hands. I admitted my faults. I made the list. I don't see how I can make direct amends to people—someone alive has to do that. If it's dying she's worried about, well, it only takes a second to die. Less than a second. That's easy. It's the time before that— the minute, the hour, the months, the lifetime—that's what's hard. And for her, ze moeten haasten.

* * *

Lily continued, "A person needs more in life than food and shelter and clothing, and all that, even more than love and spirituality. What about friends? What about just having a good time?" The other two considered this. "Chime, the other day, I can't remember when, but recently, you couldn't believe we let Jolie go. Or possibly-Jolie. Doesn't matter. She's at the party. She invited us. Don't you want to see her? To see?"

"What do you think, Gram?" said Chime.

"It's your party," he said. "It's up to you."

"I think we can call it our party now," said Chime.

So they went to the party, emerging stiff-muscled from the car, and telling themselves it was from sitting in it for so long. The archery range was an open field surrounded by trees, with a blazing bonfire set in the middle. Seen from above, concentric circles –

the ring of fire, the colorful undulating ring of people around it, a dotted ring of tents and tables and kegs and roasting hogs and vats of corn, the wide ring of green, and then the protective ring of trees against the late golden light. Self-contained, like a story within a story within a story. Guitar-heavy music vibrated through the circles and echoed back from the trees. Even sound respected the perimeter.

"Now this is what I'm talking about," said Lily. They wandered among the group, where they didn't know anyone, except that they knew everyone. Like in a dream, all the faces were familiar, the names nebulous. After David's father passed away, he took Chime to a party like this one, in a dream. He wore the blue windbreaker he had always worn in life, and she asked him what it was like to be dead. He said it was a lot like life, that you were responsible for your own happiness. Is there a heaven or a hell? No, he said. What happens, then, when you die? He said it would be difficult to explain, and Chime said please try. So he took her to a party, like this one, where all the people she had ever known were gathered. She looked around in earnest and found Dave Sr. on the other side of the crowd in the blue windbreaker. Yet he also remained next to her. And she wondered if to die were like meeting oneself at a party. Chime had a strange sensation that she could be dreaming or dead even now. He had said that death was a lot like life, and this place was certainly imbued with life.

"Gram," she started, but then shook her head, chiding herself for such thoughts. She knew what Gram would say. He'd performed this service thousands of times throughout her life, assuring her that everything was real, solid, and staunchly causative. He would say that we are superior to the animals, because as perceptual beings, they could not grasp the concept of time. Their entire awareness amounted to here, now, this. But as conceptual beings, we have great capacity to imagine. We can remember events, reimagine them to meet our emotional needs, remember dreams we swear occurred in reality, envision the future, think about a future in which we remember the past, or a past in which we dreamed of the future. We experience déjà vu and premonitions. We can carry on simultaneous relationships and harbor conflicting emotions and opinions—all remarkable ways that our consciousness deals with time. The stuff of our own heads can seem like fantasy, and it is normal to hold some confusion in the vastness of consciousness. How fantastically simple, she thought. Here, now, this. Perhaps she could make up her own mind now. She decided, yes, this was real. Here, now, this. But if she happened to encounter herself among the crowd, what then?

Chime beside another fire, on a hilltop in Iowa with Bernadette and Riggsy, Sunny asleep on her lap, and above them a sky so full of stars they held the night to a dark blue with purple edges. Riggsy had told the story of how he became the sheriff of Jackson County, and now he stirred the fire with a stick.

"This is what I want for her," Chime said. "To play softball outside until it's too dark to see the ball anymore, and then to fall asleep under a sky where you can actually see the stars. It's too hot in Memphis, and she's never seen the stars until tonight."

"That's what we wanted for our Bella, too. You will take a step backward in time when you move to Iowa, but it'll be worth it," said Bernadette. "You will have lots of friends here." Chime in the craft room, teaching Italian to the kids:

"You mean we can't just call it the shitter?" said Chad.

"No," said Chime, "God, no. You will say *bagno*. Or *doccia* if you want to take a shower."

"Can we drink alcohol in Italy?" Desi asked.

"We'll see," said Chime. So it was true, what they say. She really had become her parents, who rarely said yes or no in her childhood, but always I suppose and we'll see. What was next, zippering her coat? Warshing her hands in the zink?

"Sunny and I will do all the ordering at restaurants," said Coco, their arms linked.

"We'll starve to death!" said Desi.

And there were possibly-Jug and possibly-Karen, their parents, standing near one of the beer kegs and talking to another familiar couple, and Chime swore she heard possibly-Karen mention Chad. That Chad and his wife were coming for a visit with the grandchildren and bringing that great big dog Karen pretends not to like, whose name she pretends not to know. Chime and David, delivering a gift to Bella, when she was still in high school. She took it quickly, blushing red, and said, "You're so dumb," and that's when they knew they had been accepted, because in Iowa, often regarded as the most literate in state in America, dumb is the deepest expression of endearment. A close second would be a drunk Jug and Riggsy leaving a fifteen-minute voicemail message for David at his office, spouting their views on a variety of subjects, including beer, working too much, and David's position as CEO of a successful company, interjected with shouts of, "Chime, get your top back on! Geez! What'll Dave think?" and excessive giggling. Did Chime think David would be mad, they asked her afterward, and she said she didn't know, that no one had ever done such a thing before. You could always count on Iowans to tell you you were full of shit, that you weren't as important as you imagined, that your flaws were hilarious, and usually, to seal it with a nickname. It wove you into a big bale of Midwestern hay and set you down in the barn with the others. It made you dry, and it made you humble, and it made you normal, and it made you one of them. Whenever Lily thought she might have written THE song, Sunny and Coco would squelch such delusions of fame with "surround sound," which was the two of them running round her, making weird gestures and singing her own song back to her in exaggerated tones. The older she became, the more her sensitive ears showed their negative side, and "surround sound" was number four on the List of Auditory Annoyances Lily kept on her phone.

10. Cracking body parts.

9. Screeching like dying birds.

8. Beyonce.

7. "Harmonies."

6. Making up words to songs because they don't actually know the words.

5. Pretending to know the words to songs, but actually mimicking me.

4. "Surround sound."

3. Exaggerated southern accents and "y'all."

2. Matching pitch with the refrigeration motors at the grocery store.

1. Singing all my most favorite songs off key on purpose.

This last, she never told the girls, annoyed and amazed her equally, because she knew it was as hard to sing off pitch continuously as to sing on pitch, perhaps harder. But she wanted them to know for themselves that they were talented, not from adult praise. Could that have been her own mother's reasoning? And this, Chime realized, walking through the party, must be what she had forgotten. Lily was right, a life without friends is a life unrealized. She must thank her, she thought. But Lily was off in the crowd, talking to a group who looked like Stump and Sheryl, their children, and grandchildren. They exalt you at the same time they humble you, those Iowans. Lily sang *One Day at a Time* at the annual polka mass, over Gram's atheist protests and Chime's stage fright, a song she hadn't sung in forty years, not since the Rose Garden. Just closed her eyes and sang it, the way she used to. And when she finished, when she opened her eyes in the church, a silence rang in the space of a breath, and then, something that had never happened before in St. Joseph church. Applause. Applause rose and hit the rafters and echoed to fill the sacred gathering. And all that time she thought people had responded to her voice because it had emanated from a child. But it was just her voice. She was stunned and grateful and she gathered up the attention and the applause like bundles of light. She consumed it and it made her glow. It made her real. At the party, someone near the fire turned up the volume of *Brown Eyed Girl*, and on the choruses, the crowd raised their glasses and sang Sha-la-la-la-la-la-la-la-la-la-ladee-da. Desi singing blue eyed girl to Sunny: The stone streets of Rome hushed in rain. They huddled beneath a slick black umbrella with Coco. Rain poured like prosecco into the center of the Duomo. Street vendors sold plastic ponchos in the street and Chad chided, "*Io non voglio la ponch!*" and when they returned minutes later, "*Io non voglio la ponch*—again!" and later, "*Io non voglio la ponch*— still!" The one who had fought learning Italian the most was the one doing the 'splaining. Karen and Jug sat under an awning with Chime and David, enjoying their children and drinking wine, remarking that somehow, over the last ten years, the two families had become as one.

"Now, you're going to have to at least talk to the other moms," David said to Chime just before they took Sunny to preschool. His tone was serious.

"Even if they're stupid?" It was as if Chime, not Sunny, required socialization.

"Yes." And she tried. She went to ladies' luncheons and charity fashion shows. She was regaled with feasts of gossip and speculation, of every particulate matter that could be scattered across a surface. She learned that a "spotter" was a spider and that planes were chronically "light." She learned that women flipped the corners of peoples' rugs to see the price tags and judge their own husbands' adequacy accordingly. Are you leaving your price tags on, honey, 'cause we're looking! Hahaha. And why is your house so full of naked people, Miss Chime? Oh, you mean the art, Chime would say. We like nudes. Well I should say! You know, sugar, those tests don't mean a thing. It was a chromosomal analysis, Chime would say. She has two x chromosomes. She's a girl. Well don't you count on it now! You do have her registered at Edwards Academy, of course. And which nanny service brought you that adorable Mexican? Chella's not from a service, Chime would say, she's from El Salvador. Oh no, ma'm, we don't have black patent leather shoes that small. Y'all up north might go for that sort of thing, but we don't wear black patent until first grade. You can take that to the bank. At the end of the day she wiped it off like makeup. Eventually, though, we become what we consume, and no amount of reading Faulkner was able to explain or clear Chime's palate of that indigestible present, now past. Sunny at five: "Mommy, Bella is going to bring my new Iowa friends when she babysits me today, Coco—she's a girl, like me, and Desi—he's a boy and he's old, like nine or something, and the other boy, the one who is nice to me, and he's really old, and we're going to build a fort."

"Not a lot of friends for us between Iowas, were there," said Gram, catching Chime's elbow.

"I came to think it was us," said Chime. "That we just weren't friend material. I found it hard to trust people."

"Speak for yourself. I am nothing if not friendly fabric."

"Oh my God, while I've been reminiscing, you've been drinking."

"Why not? I feel lighter than a leaf, I could disappear any minute, I can't explain it, and I don't care."

"I've been saying that for years, except for the not caring. I care very much." She nodded toward Lily, who had now sat down to a euchre game with possibly-Stump and possibly-Sheryl.

"Tell me the story about Lily and the Engelman Band, Gram."

"Lily has to do that."

"OK, then another story."

"All right. I can be drunk and philosophical at the same time. Listen and be provoked! A frog is about to cross a stream . . . let's say an Iowa crick. A frog is about to cross a crick and a scorpion asks if he can hitch a ride on the frog's back. And the frog says hey, what's a scorpion doing in the cold Midwest . . ."

"Gram, really."

"OK, OK, he he. The scorpion asks if he can hitch a ride on the frog's back and the frog says no, you will sting me. The scorpion argues if I sting you, we both will die, and I want to cross the crick, so I won't sting you. So the frog agrees to carry the scorpion, and in midstream, the scorpion stings the frog, dooming them both. The frog asks why did you sting me and the scorpion says it is my nature to do so."

"I know the story. People will always act according to their nature, even against their own self-interest."

"That's the moral of the story, yes, but it's not my point."

"Are we the frog in the story, and the people we meet the scorpion?"

"No, no. Listen. I feel like I don't have a lot of time to make my sentient points here. So just listen."

"Salient."

"What?"

"Salient points. You said sentient."

"See? Not much time. My point is that that's not the original story. It was told in the Babylonian Talmud, and there, the scorpion makes it across the stream and stings a man on the other side. Another story, which could be even older, says the scorpion makes it across the stream and saves a man from being bitten by something else. The frog is never even harmed. In other versions, the frog is a tortoise and scorpion stings him but his shell protects him from harm."

"Interesting."

"What I'm saying is that the story has been rewritten. Stories get rewritten."

"I can imagine that the frog has a thing or two to say from his perspective. He gets a bad rap in the current version."

"Yes. Someone with a dark view of existence made changes. And now . . . well, I can't remember what I planned to say after the story, but . . . rewrite. That's important. Rewrite, Chime."

They drank all the Rumchata, and when that ran out, they drank beer. The crackling fire and rising voices, and rock and roll joined to create one continuous song, with accents of laughter and

"You're shittin' me!" and "Looks like you're euchred, my friend!" And they decided that all these strangers with familiar faces were in fact the people they resembled, and the three began calling them by the names they knew. As the party progressed, it didn't seem to matter, because they all had become friends anyway. Gram found them to be like characters in a novel who represented real people known to the writer, given pseudonyms to protect the fiction. For elipses of time he even felt as though he were the writer, creating reality from rarified ether. He initiated several conversations with those around him about the godlike nature of creating and naming, his inebriated state keeping his normally polysyllabic discourse to a minimum. He cracked jokes about the irony of his own name. He smiled handsomely and listened and nodded with enthusiasm. He laughed fully. In short, he became the extrovert he could have been all along, was born to be. Goodbye, backward and shy Gram, Chime said to herself. She felt tired, as she always did when she drank, but more so this time. Maybe because they had been traveling for so long. Tired and content and present. She was grateful for a sweatshirt when someone handed them out, because it was getting colder. The trees had swallowed the sun, but in its stubborn refusal to die it burst forth from their leaves like fire. The inner ring of fire and the outer ring of trees radiated in similar hues. Nothing ever dies as long as people can gather and talk about the past. We become what we consume and, for Iowans, even those who are not farmers, it spills out again in rural metaphors. Unhook the plow. Your cows are getting out. A bunch of biting sows. Tough as a cob. Lily had the best time of all, because she had always been able to make connections with people on a level deeper than names and faces. She punctuated her winning euchre tricks by pounding the cards down on the table in a take-that!-and-that!- and-that! maneuver, just like Smitty had done when he was younger. And now she was over by the Engelman Band, tuning a guitar, getting ready to play, instead of telling their story. But time is short, so allow me.

"I have to run home and get my horn," said Cougar. "It's out at the farmhouse. They want me to play tonight."

"I'll come with you," said Lily, and they drove out of town and up across the ridge named after his family and past all his brothers' farms. Cougar showed her where his land began and he apologized for the condition of his ditches, which were neatly mowed and sprinkled with wildflowers. Lily complimented him on the water breaks in the fields, knowing that the engineering of his farm land would be a source of pride, despite that she knew nothing about water breaks. In the barnyard, a farm dog, as old and kind as Cougar himself, greeted them.

"There she is," he sang, as they got out of the car. "There's Betsy. How are you, Betsy? Is everything fine on the farm?" And then, to Lily, "This is Betsy. She takes care of this place."

"Oh, I love her," said Lily, kneeling to hug the dog. Cougar told her how many head of cattle he fed every day, how many new calves had been born, and how Betsy helped him with the chores. He and his wife had a house in town, down by the river, but eighty-three-year-old Cougar drove out to the farm twice a day to tend to the cattle and to feed Betsy. This appeared to be an agreeable arrangement to Betsy, for she swayed her shoulders and tail and waited good naturedly while he stepped inside the farmhouse to grab his saxophone. It was fitting that he play the saxophone, like his father, Ambrose Sr. When Amby's death left a wife and twelve children, his sons vowed to keep all the entertainment gigs he had booked, so they took up instruments as necessary, from the youngest, Stump, who was four years old, to Cougar, the oldest, who was twenty. Calling themselves the Valleymen, they made good on every booking, and then just kept on going. When Lily moved back to Iowa and met the Engelmans, they were sixty years into the gig. But they had seen each other before they met, for the Engelman boys used to have supper once in a while at the Rose Garden back in the 1970s, where they were entertained by a young singer whose name they didn't know. Lily once saw an old photograph of the family, taken just before Ambrose, Sr. passed away, Cougar standing proudly in the back row, sharply dressed and good looking and ready for action. That's how he feels on the inside, even now, thought Lily and she decided that image was what she would see whenever she looked at him. So you see, faces were not nearly as important as souls in Lily's world, and this circle of familiar strangers at the bonfire was no different from any other audience. While she was performing, and Gram was extroverting, Jolie found Chime in the crowd.

"Hey!" she said, "I'm glad you guys came!" as if she had expected Chime. "Look what I found whilst shopping for rum," and she held out the book. THE book. Leather cover, shrinking weight, full of words everywhere, except where you are. "Stupidly, I left HyVee forgetting to buy rum, so, of course, I ran back to get some, and this was on the shelf. Imagine! Between Rumchata and its uglier cousin, Rico's." While Jolie talked, Chime juggled several thoughts at once. First, nobody outside of England used the word whilst, except Jolie and herself. They had always joked that it would be their identifying word in case either was kidnapped and held for ransom. Jolie, with a gun to her head would say yes, they took me whilst I was jogging, and Chime would know it was really her. Second, Jolie hadn't seen Chime at the grocery store, so Chime hadn't been included in her invitation. Third, and this thought made the others trivial by comparison, she was holding out the book for Chime to take. Lily must have left it, accidentally or on purpose, in the store. Considering her own last encounter with the book, Chime was afraid to take it.

"Thank you. Yes, that's mine. Ours. Would you mind just setting it right here near me? Then I won't have to expose my hands to the cold." She tucked her hands further into her sleeves.

"Well if you're cold, c'mon, let's move closer to the fire." Jolie moved back to Iowa when her kids were grown. It gets into you, and it calls you back. Her first romantic relationship back home failed. Sunny was ten when that date first pulled up the driveway.

"Aunt Jolie, your date's here! Hide!" As always, Sunny was full of unrecognized wisdom. Iowa is not just a pretty face. She requires work. Neglected, she reverts to wilderness. To the Mississippi uncontained and the bluffs lifting their chins against it. To unrelenting weeds and turkey vultures. To snow and snow and snow. To times past. To trappers and fur traders and Meskwaki scouts. To the Sauk and Black Hawk, the Ioway and the Illinois.

To Marquette and Joliet. Julien Dubuque is not buried in his grave, Smitty says. The Indians threw him off the bluff into the river just near the site where his monument stands, he says, and it doesn't matter whether Smitty is young or old when he recounts this, because the story is immortal, and then he spits a watermelon seed onto the ground, and there, a watermelon vine takes hold and strangles weaker foliage.

10

Legacy, according to the dictionary, is something from the past, bequeathed forward, or something in the present, inherited from the past, or something outdated— that is, out of time. And so it was with the book, which Jolie continued to carry as she and Chime moved closer to the fire. It was a shame that Chime could not physically hold the book, because word mysteries like the ones it contained had always consumed her. *Enough* implied too much. *Soon* always occurred later. *Then* was at that time but also soon after that, and then some. *Now* was at the present time, and the time immediately before the present, and the time immediately to follow, or sometimes, or used with the sense of presentness entirely lost. *Yet* hadn't quite happened or was still happening. *Time* denoted anything at all. On time, in time, at times, over time, time out, time's up, frequently, repeatedly, on schedule, on the installment plan, sufficiently early, eventually, in correct tempo, very quickly or soon, leisurely, occasionally, for the present, at intervals, nevertheless, yet, a rate, a measurement, a season, an era, an age, a beat, an occasion, a duration, a turn, finite, infinite.

"I'm not eating my toast. I hate it."

"Jocelyn, don't say hate," Chime told her at seven years old. "Make your verbs interesting. Say loathe." They were in Sunny's kitchen at breakfast and a smile spread across Sunny's face, as she remembered hearing the same advice some thirty years before. Jocelyn left a note on the counter before she left for school: "Dear Grammy, I loathe bread. I loave bread. I love bread. Love, Jocelyn." Chime tucked this note into her wallet, next to the one that said, "You are the gradis mommy in the world. I love you. Love, Sunny." And now she stood near the bonfire with Jolie and someone announced that the hogs were ready, and the crowd swarmed the food tables. Lily and Gram came over and greeted Jolie as if they had known her for years.

"Where'd you get that?" he asked Jolie, indicating the book.

"I found it in the grocery store when I went back for rum," she said. Gram turned to Lily, who made one attempt at lying and then gave up.

"Look, it's been following us around for this whole trip," Lily said. "And it was kind of fun, at first, weeks ago, but lately it's been causing my companions some trouble." She looked at her companions for agreement, but they were silent. The three had never discussed sharing their experience with others. Lily took their silence as a desire for continued secrecy, so she said,

"Oh alright. Give it to me. Thank you for returning our book." Jolie handed her the book and Lily raised her eyebrows to the other two, as if to ask if they were satisfied.

"I think I'm going to get something to eat," said Jolie, sensing the tension. "I'll talk to you guys later." And then, to Lily, "Beautiful songs, by the way." She left the three of them standing at the fire.

"Lily, what the hell?" said Gram, grabbing the book from her. His head, which was already spinning from the beer, added somersaults to the ride. Either his feet were not under him, or they were near to sliding out ahead of him, he wasn't sure. He staggered.

Lily took back the book and said, "This is what I'm talking about. And it's why I left this thing in the store. Good riddance, I say. We don't need it."

"Maybe we don't need it," said Chime, "but I'd like to keep it with us."

"As would I," said Gram.

"That is, if you don't mind carrying it a while longer," said Chime. "What time is it?"

Lily, singing a note for thirty seconds: "And that's how it's done," she said to the students, though it was amazing she had any breath left with which to speak.

"I can't hold a note for that long," said her young protégé.

"Of course you can," said Lily. "You're just not there yet. I'll show you some exercises to increase your lung capacity and some techniques for releasing the air while maintaining pitch. You'll be great on the stage!" They rehearsed in the music room that bore her name and musical ideology.

"But my lungs are tiny. I'm only twelve and you're, like, forty-five." That's right, Lily thought. Tell all your friends. She wore black leggings and a long, knit tunic and separate shirtcollar necklace, and heels. Lily was seventy. And still, the songs came to her in her sleep. Paul McCartney came again in a dream, and she hugged him tight and he asked why she would not let him go. She was afraid it might be his last visit, and she wanted to write just one song, that one great song. Don't worry, love, you will write it. We'll write it together. And she lived for the promise. Sunny, at forty: "Well, I guess I'm going to have to be a writer, so that books don't suck."

"The Sunny I raised spoke with more eloquence at three," said Chime. "Who are you?"

"That was before cynicism and I got a room together in the wasteland of literature. We're thinking of having sarcasm and satire over for drinks."

"Ahh, there she is."

Smitty, at ninety-nine: "How old would you be if you didn't know how old you were?" One farmer's philosophy. Daniel pushed his siblings to move him into a nursing home. He thinks there are people in the trees, you know, Daniel said. Chime went out to the cabin and sat with him on the porch, holding the fumey homemade wine in a jelly glass. Made from cherries, peppers, and elderberries. The peppers give it a kick, don't you think? And there was a robin Smitty swore had returned for the tenth year in a row. Who knew that robins lived so long or why they always came back to the same place. He was of the land. And the land was of him. He would die here, three hundred yards from where he was born, the sum of himself and the land encompassing so much more than the two. He wanted to be outside, perhaps to fall quietly into his garden and be covered over with leaves. And Chime looked up the hill toward the old farmhouse, where he had been born, and she had been born, and saw the faces. In the trees. Abraham Lincoln with a leafy, disproportionate stovepipe hat and Albert Einstein minus one eye, and a dog, whose left ear moved up and down when the wind stirred. She smiled. And she traced then where her creativity had come from, and marveled at its profuse blossoming in Sunny and now Jocelyn. Sunny, at three, had lain on his chest. "I'm counting his whiskers!" she announced. He lived long enough to hear Jocelyn call him Pa Mitty. And, one final time, his name changed. Jocelyn, in little blonde braids, with Sunny and Desi in Amsterdam. She had mastered one defensive Dutch sentence, *Ik spreek geen Nederlands*, I speak no Dutch, but it didn't seem to matter. Shopkeepers, bellboys, and taxi drivers spoke to her in Dutch as if she were one of them, her looks belying her words. As if she were a diminutive tour guide escorting the American couple.

A light, but cold rain fell onto Derby Grange, and Chime, Gram, and Lily crowded under the tents with the rest of the partiers. Lily heaped a plate with roasted pork and buttered corn and warm German potato salad. She ate as if for the first time in days, which indeed is how it seemed to her. Gram tried to eat, but food made him queasy, and Chime now knew better than to try. Chime watched out at the rain falling into the fire and listened for sizzles, but if any sounded, they were lost in the increasing party volume. The rain seemed to energize, rather than dampen, the general spirit of the occasion. A five-month-old Sunny sat at the patio door and cried to go outside. It had been raining softly and steadily in Memphis for three days, and finally, Chime strapped the baby to her chest, got an umbrella, and walked through the neighborhood in the rain. And that tiny baby shouldn't be out in this rain, Miss Chime. Thank you, Miss Milly. I'll take her inside straight away. Turned the corner out of Miss Milly's sight and kept going. Chime sang raindrops keep fallin' on my head and singin' in the rain and rain on me and I do my cryin' in the rain and purple rain and have you ever seen the rain and fool in the rain and rainy days and Mondays and when she ran out of pop songs she made up a song about Sunny in the rain. And Sunny was content. Está contenta, Chella would say. Chime and Sunny got caught in a sudden downpour when Sunny was two, and Chime lifted the bulk of her sweatshirt for Sunny to climb in. Mother and daughter shared the wide neck hole, and that time they sang together, while whipping their dripping hair at each other. Sunny and Desi, at six and ten, stood in an Iowa summer deluge, washing their hair with shampoo from the pool house, while all the parents looked on from the cabana, amused. Sunny wished then that it would rain on her wedding day and later her wish came true.

Looking past the fire and the tables and into the green space of the archery range, which was now celadon in rain and dusk, Chime watched a young man with a longbow set up a straw target and pace a distance away from it. He turned about face, and, in the worst possible conditions for field archery, drew an arrow with his bowstring and aimed for the target. For a second he shone silver against the trees, like lightning, then he released the arrow toward its goal.

"Do you see that out there, Gram?" she said. "Somebody is out in the field with a bow."

"My vision fails me for distance," said Gram. "I would have to switch to my other glasses."

"When did you get glasses?"

"2019."

"What time did you just say it was?"

"I said it was late. The rain is freezing. And we need to talk with Lily now."

"Yes. Yes, I suppose we do." They pulled Lily from a beer-fueled conversation with some other musicians about the current state of popular music. Then the three, bundled on the outside in hooded sweatshirts, light with alcohol on the inside, and one of them fed, resumed their journey. They decided to walk beyond the circle of people and tents and tables, beyond the trees and up the hill to the recreation clubhouse, where it would be private and dry. Rain mixed with tiny shards of ice and tinkled like crystal on the trees. Chime couldn't remember whose idea this outing had been, this diversion to bring them together, but she remembered it had seemed extremely important—vital, in fact. She also felt that it would be ending soon and she would welcome a rest. Walking was warming her, but she knew that as soon as she stopped, she wouldn't be able to fend off the cold. The farm had been on a hill like this. She walked it every day, after the school bus dropped her off. In winter, she raced behind Kitsy and Daniel to the bottom on sleds, and on those occasions the walking up didn't seem like such a chore. On Sundays after church, in the mud or snow, Smitty would pile all the kids in the back seat for better traction, and come at the lane from the east side to get a good run at it. Put it in gear and everybody hang on. The old car would spin and lurch up the hill, mud or snow splattering out behind the wheels, and Smitty maneuvering the steering wheel with singular intensity and jamming the accelerator to the floorboards. They would keep going until the car stalled in a whining spin on the steepest of the incline and ceased to move forward, and Smitty would back the vehicle all the way down to the bottom and start again. It was a challenge for him, this poorly maintained lane, part of his lifelong effort to conjure more from the land than what it so beguilingly promised, and he never gave up. He either made it to the top, which was rare, or after numerous attempts the family sighed and groaned and begged to walk the rest of the way, in the mud or snow, in their church clothes. Chime's subconscious noted to always have pretty, clean shoes when she grew up. And yet, it was those rare conquests of the lane that made more indelible memories, when the whole family would break into victorious cheering and spill from the car and bound up the steps of home. Again, she lived in a big house on a hill, when she returned to live in Iowa with David and Sunny. Again, she walked it daily, though the intervening years had removed all but the cardiovascular challenge from such a climb. In winter, she raced Sunny, Coco, Desi, and Chad to the bottom on inflatable saucers and told them the story of how the original owner of the house was killed in a horse and buggy accident on the driveway, at the very spot where they were launching their races, but two hundred years earlier. And Sunny told Jocelyn the story of how her Great, Great, Great, Great, Great Grandpa Smith pulled the rocks from the ground and transformed the wilderness of that other hill into a farm and how her Pa Mitty made hay on the hillside with a team of horses in his youth and a high-tech super baler later. How his family ate only bread and sorghum for two years during the Depression and how he made homemade wine in his cabin on the front forty acres and charged the lane on a muddy Sunday. And so everything lived, and would live, as long as there were hills to be conquered and stories to tell. In her reverie, Chime didn't know if she were traversing the hill from the first years of her life or from the last years. In dreams, she was always mowing one hill or the other, grooming, keeping the weeds at bay.

Lily startled her with, "So, what are we doing after we get off of this peace train, guys?" Chime and Gram searched each other's widened eyes through the rain for an answer, but none materialized. "Or, why don't we just take the long way . . . 'cause I'm having a really good time."

"I think we have to talk about a couple of things, still," said Chime, hesitant.

"Oh I know, I know, the Willa thing. It wouldn't be my first choice. But I know it's important to you. Maybe when we get up top we can cozy up in front of a fire, an indoor fire, and do that."

"Yes. I'm tired."

"As am I," said Gram.

"You know," said Lily, without registering her companions' condition, "You would think I would get tired of playing the old songs with all the old guys, but I don't." They trudged uphill and she continued. "Do you know how hard it is, what kind of skill it takes, to play the trumpet, or the saxophone, like Cougar? I think I'm going to take up the trumpet." She strode with determination in the freezing rain, the book tucked up under her sweatshirt, keeping herself from pulling ahead of the others.

"Anything else?" said Gram.

"Well, as long as I'm moving into the brass family, I guess sax and trombone would be the natural progression, but I'm not very familiar with valved instruments. The French horn is quite advanced, I know. I had a boyfriend in high school who—"

"For God's sake, Lily, can you talk about anything else?" That was Chime, who suddenly found someone to blame for her discomfort—and not just in the present moment, but (as she was about to discover), always. Her whole life.

"Chime, maybe you shouldn't"— Gram started.

"No. I should. We're almost out of time. Lily, does every last second have to be about you and music?" Lily kept walking but her elevated mood halted.

"If you mean generally, then, yes. Every second of my life tends to be intimately related to me. Imagine. And my life is music." Lily let the tinkling rain sound the percussive accents to this song.

"Lily, maybe it would be better if—" Gram tried again.

"Oh pipe down, Gramophone," she said. "Here, why don't you carry the book and we'll see what would be better." She had meant to be funny, but mention of the book brought a melancholy that fell on them colder than the rain. A silence between them was counted by the rhythm of the sleet. Then Lily sighed and said, "You guys, I meant it. I've been having a good time and I don't feel tired and I don't feel old, and I don't know what else to do other than what I've always done. Write some more songs and sing them and learn some more." She waited for a response, but Chime and Gram continued walking, silently. "I'm happy for you, Gram. So happy that you seem to have found some peace and got to play in the leaves and come to some sort of understanding. It's beautiful. If I were you, I'd write that novel now." Gram nodded slightly, but still no response from Chime. "And Chime, you'll be free of that voice in your head—the one that sounds a lot like Willa—when we get home—er, to the top of this hill, whatever, when we talk it out. But I don't have some major issue to reconcile." This struck Chime as the oddest thing to say. Gram had met his epiphany and this should be the time for Lily to do likewise. They were running out of time.

"What about your need to be famous?" Chime said, finally. "What about never becoming the one thing you had talent for, the one thing you knew since you were three years old you wanted to be?"

"Are you kidding? I'd be desperate and broke somewhere, with a trail of husbands and tears and vodka bottles behind me. I said back in the 80s, when we went back to school, that I would always love music, but not the music business, remember?"

"I thought that was a . . . self-deception."

"Nope."

"But I thought . . . You always say you're waiting for that one song, the one that will make you famous."

"You don't think there's a chance for that, at our age, do you?" said Gram, incredulous.

"But Mother always said that I . . ."

"If I were you," said Lily, "I would have turned that into a song years ago. You know, sing it out into the world and let it survive on the air that's out there instead of living like a parasite in your head. But that's you." Chime began to move her head back and forth in a slow motion "no" and Lily went on. That's how you're put together. Like Gram is wired for words and I'm made for music. But you don't have an outlet like we do. Such a creative mind, with no outlet for it. No, Chime's head repeated. And the things you let in here! No. And the rain came down on them. The sadness you invite. The darkness. No. That voice that tells you everything you do is wrong. No. We almost lost David because of it, remember? No. The rain quickened. You get in a story in your head and you imagine it's real. No. Because you don't know where the boundaries are. No. Rain and rain. And you drag me into it and make my songs sad. No. And you let that voice in and you let it tear Gram apart. No. And he has to put everything back together, so he can't possibly create or have any fun. No. I remember clothes and music; Gram remembers words. What do you remember? Every time someone hurt you? Every single slight? No, I . . . And what would have become of Sunny? No. Please. You would have let her life fall apart so you could use the line 'And I'm the saddest person in the world' at the end of a sonnet! No, I was surviving . . . For iambic pentameter! I couldn't . . . Your greatest value for the right pissin' number of syllables! What is wrong with this picture, Chime?

"No! I've changed my mind." They were at the steepest part of the hill, at the place where the car either made it up or slid backwards, the place from whence the kids launched, the place where an old man in a story lost his life. Chime said, "I've changed my mind. I don't want to do this anymore," and the three stopped.

"Except that you do," said Gram, because here we are. Chime was crying, but you couldn't tell because of the rain. "I didn't know. How could I have known? I thought Lily . . . Lily was the one."

"I've always done exactly what I wanted to do," Lily said gently.

"I've always done what I had to do," said Gram.

"And I'm the one who made it so difficult," said Chime. "So needlessly difficult." She turned her face upward and the sleet melted into her tears. "I thought I was doing the best I could," she said, though it was unclear who she was talking to just then. Had you seen them in the moments after that, maybe had you been that autumnal archer out in the field, you would have seen three small dots of light at the top of the hill that the rain seemed to variously wash into one larger dot and back into three, ascending the steps of home.

11

The sleet persisted across eastern Iowa, but inside, a fire held the house in a warm embrace. In the living room there was a stone hearth and a bronze mantelpiece in the figure of a goat that began in smooth hooves at the floor on each side, rising up in muscled legs and shouldering the mantel and the goat's horned head. Its expression was one of fierce, bearded determination, and it was original to the structure. Two centuries had faded the house into a rural legend by the time they moved back to Iowa, but more time and diligent work and creative taste had restored it even beyond its former glory. For most of the two hundred years, its inhabitants did without a permanent kitchen. Servants cooked over a giant hearth in the cellar and served in the formal dining room. Various first floor rooms were converted to makeshift kitchens in the twentieth century, but none prevailed. A kitchen addition in the 1950s was partially destroyed in a fire, and by the time five-year-old Sunny skipped through the halls singing Our house! Our house! the kitchen was a disheveled remnant of that midcentury attempt. Chime instructed the contractors to remove the wall that separated the kitchen from the main part of the house, and to enlarge the room to a full conservatory, with a high, slanting glass roof and expansive glass walls to let in the vibrant view and the sunlight reflected off the Mississippi River. It became the heart of the house, and from that magnificent space she served her family. She made pot roast and pies and lit candles and vased flowers. At Christmas, she decorated a tree in every room and constructed a grand gingerbread house with Sunny, powdered sugar floating like their laughter through the kitchen. She shopped and wrapped and brined and baked, and gave care to proportion, line, and space. She attended to the senses, to the effect of memories, for she was their entertainment and their author. And in making the home, she became home. She understood, then, that her efforts would define the word for Sunny. Only much later did she understand that the root of home was not in a physical structure, no matter how safe and comfortable, and not merely an atmosphere, no matter how loving, but a resonance in the mind. For Sunny, one that whispered like wind and wound like a brook in Chime's own voice. And as much as the mother wanted authorial control over it, the daughter would edit it as she pleased, or as she feared, with her own experience. And Chime came to think, at the same time, if only it worked differently, and thank goodness it works that way. How would she wish that heaven had left her still, the whispering zephyr, and the purling rill? Who finds not Providence all good and wise, alike in what it gives and denies? Chime, at 58, somewhere she thought she might never be: The Italian orchestra in the cruise ship's main dining room played David's Eyes as a surprise she had arranged. David took her hand and led her to the dance floor. It had been five years, one month, and eighteen days since he had looked at her with the love in his eyes, where she had once lived, and now, when she again became visible to him, she said, "David, you're back," and lived once more, and for the rest of their time together, in his eyes.

She didn't know what he saw when he looked at her that way, except that it was a completeness. As if all things were hers to choose and came into being exactly as she wished. Others looked and saw a fashion church, and a poet, loud and scattered, and writing songs in her sleep, and she knew they saw only Lily. Some saw a shy and awkward bookworm, and she knew they saw only Gram. Many saw the consummate mother, and few, a quivering child under her skirts.

The three had changed into dry lounging clothes and pajamas, and Lily had deposited the book on a table in the other room, and they sat before the goated fireplace, sipping hot tea. Grandma Vanderbeek already had started them on weak tea with milk and sugar at five years old, in the old Dutch custom. Three generations later, Jocelyn ordered iced tea with milk at a restaurant in Dubuque and the waiter omitted the milk because surely she was mistaken. In Amsterdam, milk for tea was brought for Jocelyn without being ordered, which saved her from having to explain, in perfect Dutch, that she spoke no Dutch. The tradition of St. Nicholas Day also survived, Jocelyn placing her shoes outside her bedroom door on the eve of December fifth as receptacles for candy. And her joy was not diminished at all by knowing it was Sunny who delivered the candy. Gram made sure no lies were told to children, and Lily made sure there were pretty shoes for all.

"Remember when Willa used to say putfutiapin or something like that and tell us it was a Dutch word?

"It could have been *put je voet een hoppin*, put your foot a hoppin. Maybe an expression of urgency."

"So maybe she didn't make it up, after all."

"I don't think she was good at making things up."

"She looked to us for that."

"Now that you mention it, we did contribute a bit to her night school classes over the years. Whenever she needed something creative."

"Remember Spanish 101?"

"She wanted so much to speak Spanish."

"Yes, but she was, what, forty? That window was closed."

"Forty is when we became fluent. It's possible."

"Thanks to Chella's inability to speak English."

"And a good ear. There's a lot to be said for a good ear. You can't say something if you can't hear it. Just like you can't play something if you can't hear it."

"She wanted to play the piano, too."

"And she looked to us for that, as well."

"It seems like we did everything that she had wanted to do."

"By the time we came along, we must have been a gift."

"A gift."

"Hmm."

"I had to spend the day in her classroom once, for some reason. I must have been two or three. Thick books, chalkboards, kids everywhere, fawning over me like a pet. I hit my chin on the bookcase and started crying, and she took me out into the hall and comforted me. I wanted to stay there, in the hallway, all day."

"She held me on her lap during a meeting in the back of church. I put my head against her chest and listened to the sound of her voice on the inside. I had blue shorts on."

"She taught me fractions when I was failing math at school."

"She and Dad took me to a park somewhere. Again, I must have been two or three . I don't know where the siblings were, but it was a wonderful day with just the three of us. They watched me go down the slide."

"She liked the flowers Kitsy and I chose for her funeral."

"I remember smelling her perfume suddenly—"

"And then the image of the flowers, yes. She always tried to grow roses, remember?"

"She taught me to count to ten in Dutch."

"Once, she read my stories."

"She taught me old songs and we would sing them in the car on the way home, and she always let me take the harmonies. She could sing."

"She loved words."

"She pretended for me that Truly was real."

"She had some kick-ass high-heeled pumps and a shiny black satin blouse back in the day."

"She tutored students, even after she retired. She must have been good at it."

"I remember a day when she seemed happy. We were all out in the yard after supper and she did cartwheels with us on the grass."

"Yes, and once she came and sat on our bed in the morning and we talked."

"I remember! And once she said I might be a good writer someday."

"Yes! And once she laughed when she read one of my stories."

"And once she listened to me play the piano."

"And once she took me by the hand."

"And once she said she loved me."

And once.

For a moment, there was an even silence. Then a part of Chime said I suppose it's time and another said yes I'm tired now. Another said I wonder what we will become. And outside, the sleet lightened and turned to snow, points of frozen light against the darkness of the sky. It set out to blanket the farmland and the silos and the barns, and make the land hard and silent and unyielding for a time. They hobbled to the bedroom, where they sensed movement and voices, real or imagined. Chime lay down on the bed with her feet stretched out in front of her and the two pulled the covers around her and leaned in close. They embraced, finally, and without fear, and Chime heard faintly, "What dumb names you gave us."

"I love you, too," she said.

12

She was perhaps dreaming, or hearing a conversation, or remembering a book, or maybe a conversation from a dream or a book; on her way somewhere, and she clutched for something. Oh, it was her pink pajamas. And her own bed where she lay. Where had she been just now? It faded so quickly, and now fingers of light reached her and stirred time.

"Hi, Mom," said Sunny. "You were asleep for a minute. You feeling OK?"

"Sunny." She reached for her.

"Yep, I'm here." Sunny took her hand.

"David . . ."

"Dad's gone, Mom. Remember?" But she couldn't remember. That part of her which had worked tirelessly to mark the boundaries between reality and imagination was now at rest. So the man who walked like he owned the world, whose sense of life inspired all her songs and all her sonnets, could exist unfettered to mortality. She had never left the promise of his eyes. David's eyes over dinner at Marché, and all else blurred. David's eyes exuding love when she entered a room. David's eyes penetrating her naked skin. David's eyes returning with love on a cruise ship. David's Eyes, Occhi del Amore, the Eyes of Love.

"Here, let's get you some water." Jocelyn brought a pitcher of water to Sunny, who poured some into a glass, and Chime raised herself to drink. She considered for a moment the image of Jocelyn and Sunny, both born under the sign of Aquarius, carrying water, and it seemed fitting. And she had read somewhere, or remembered from something, that after a spiritual awakening, one should carry a message to others, like water.

"You will listen to my songs . . ." she said to Sunny.

"Yes, always."

"And take care of my books."

"Of course." She wanted to say don't let the darkness in, don't let it feed on you. But that was her own story, not her daughter's. Sunny's story traveled a different narrative, its own climax, its own ending. Sunny herself was writing it. It would probably begin on a day when a lively rain fell on Memphis, Tennessee. And then Iowa would call for her, as it always does to its own, and she would answer.

Chime became aware of others in the room. Desi, Coco, Chad and his wife. Karen and Jug. The Engelman boys and their wives. It seemed they had been there for a while, as if she had fallen asleep in the middle of a big party that had been going on for some time. She liked that idea. Yes, a party. With food and cocktails, cards and sudden laughter. And music . An effusion of light from within, while outside the snow accumulated silently. While the farmland slept and dreamed of the next season. They came to her, one or two at a time, and said all the things that people say in parting, not realizing the verbs they chose hinged on the infinitive to be. You were always so talented. You were my musical inspiration. You are a good friend. You are the best grandmother in the whole world. You should be resting. You will be with David soon. You were. You are. You shall be.

And when they had all left the room, and it was just Sunny, she said to her mother, "You are the greatest mommy in the world. I love you." Chime took these words and folded them up into her heart where they remained. And then two things happened simultaneously to Chime and Sunny, so that each could not acknowledge the other. Chime pulled the covers up some more and looked down at her feet, which were bare, and then at the foot of the bed, where, on a table shone a pair of strappy Italian shoes, in bright yellow, with nail head trim and fringe and an artistic swoop of a heel, and next to that, a small jar of what looked like dirt. And she felt another wave of love, and smiled. Sunny picked up a book from the nightstand and turned it over. The leatherbound volume felt smooth and light in her hands. Its title, gilded and embossed, rose to meet her touch. She fanned the pages, which smelled faintly like her mother's perfume, and the book fell open to a page of ordinary words. A page which said, "The love she felt for this child overwhelmed her, mind and soul. Love poured from her. She watched every eyelash grow in, and praised every utterance. She held a secret fantasy about running away with the baby and living, just the two of them, in a small apartment, away from the world, and she was amazed by her own fantasy . . ." and Sunny knew she was reading about herself. She turned to Chime with a question on her lips. But Chime is not there. She moves through time. She moves in an old blue stock truck. In a yellow car. She moves in words, in interesting verbs. And she moves by thinking about flying. She sings, or hears herself singing, when she flies. She is humbled. She is exalted. She is made of corn, oats, and hay. Of clover. Cornstalks sprout from her sleeves. She is baled and tied with twine and fed to the cattle, which are fed to the people, which are given to time. She is an archer, aiming her arrow toward the sky, a tree, reaching for lightning, as all living things must do, in time. She is Daisy Fey in a rainbow of shirts, in joy, and in grief, in a circle of time. She is a fish, swimming upward through words, toward the light, a fish turning on her side in resignation and lifted up again by a metaphysical finger. Try. A fish eating a stick of butter. Truly. Try. And she is music. And her name sounds the time.

CPSIA information can be obtained
at www.ICGtesting.com
Printed in the USA
BVHW041046100720
583264BV00003B/329